AN EARLY WINTER

AN EARLY WINTER

by MARION DANE BAUER

CLARION BOOKS • NEW YORK

ACKNOWLEDGMENTS

With thanks to Greg Larson, my fishing expert,
and to Ann Goddard for constant support and encouragement
and to my editor, Jim Giblin, for being there still

Clarion Books • a Houghton Mifflin Company imprint • 215 Park
Avenue South, New York, NY 10003 • Copyright © 1999 by Marion
Dane Bauer • All rights reserved. • For information about permission
to reproduce selections from this book, write to Permissions, Houghton
Mifflin Company, 215 Park Avenue South, New York, NY 10003. •
Printed in the USA.

Library of Congress Cataloging-in-Publication Data

Bauer, Marion Dane.
An early winter / by Marion Dane Bauer.
p.   cm.
Summary: When eleven-year-old Tim's beloved grandfather
develops Alzheimer's disease, Tim tries to restore and save him by
taking him out for a fishing adventure at the pond, but the
outing turns into a disaster.
ISBN 0-395-90372-6
[1. Grandfathers—Fiction. 2. Alzheimer's disease—Fiction.
3. Fishing—Fiction.] I. Title.
PZ7.B3262Ear   1999
[Fic]—dc21   98-54975
CIP
AC
BP 10 9 8 7 6 5 4 3 2 1

For John Bennett Larson

CONTENTS

ONE   Going Home/1

TWO   Waiting for the Leaves to Fall/10

THREE   A Plan/21

FOUR   Gone Fishin'/32

FIVE   Making Change/41

SIX   Something to Prove/54

SEVEN   Absolutely Useless/64

EIGHT   Disaster!/77

NINE   No Choice/84

TEN   Where Are You?/92

ELEVEN   Found/101

TWELVE   Home/110

ONE

Going Home

Home," the car's tires hum against the endless asphalt. "Home!"

Home, Tim hums to himself, the word reverberating inside his head. He is tucked as far into the corner of the back seat as his seat belt will allow. *I am going home.*

Home to the two-story white house with the wraparound porch. Home to his attic room, too hot in the summer, cold in the winter, with a dormer window that opens into the limbs of the old maple. Home to his grandmother's oatmeal-raisin cookies and her lemonade, so sweet and so tart at the same time that it makes your jaws ache.

Home to Granddad. More than anything else, home to Granddad.

The insistent humming inside Tim's head is almost enough to keep the voices in the front seat from penetrating. Almost.

"We've got to face it, Paul. It's Alzheimer's. What else could be causing—"

Alzheimer's. The word leaps across the space between the front and back seats. The tires pick it up, too, and make it part of their song. *Alzheimer's. Home. Alzheimer's, Alzheimer's, Alzheimer's. Home.* Tim tugs at the restraining seat belt and twists in his seat.

Alzheimer's!

After a few moments, though, the humming repetition begins to drain the word's terrible power. *Alzheimer's* becomes just another combination of sounds. Like *asparagus.* Like *albatross.* A word that has nothing to do with him. Nothing to do with his grandfather.

This isn't the first time Tim has heard of Alzheimer's. The word had been whispered long before he and his mother ever moved from his grandparents' house in Wisconsin to Paul's apartment in Minneapolis. And his mother and Paul have talked of little else since Grandma's last call with the report from the doctor. *Alzheimer's disease.* The first time he heard his mother say it he thought she'd said *old-timer's disease.* But Granddad is only sixty-three. Everybody agrees that isn't old. Most people haven't even retired at sixty-three.

2

Besides, it doesn't matter what the doctors say. It doesn't matter how much the grownups complain about Granddad's forgetting, about all the ways they say the illness is affecting his brain. Tim knows what his grandfather's problem is. And he knows what to do about it, too.

He also knows what a dumb little kid he's been. He'd been glad when he'd found out Paul was going to marry his mother. Actually glad. Paul with the barrel chest and the open smile and the endless patience for playing catch and horse and going down when he was tackled as though he'd felt the hit. Paul with the construction job that sent him to live near them in tiny Sheldon, Wisconsin, for a whole year . . . and then, when the project he'd been working on was finished, pulled him back to Minneapolis again. And pulled Tim and his mother with him.

Tim had been dumb enough to think that Paul was going to move in with him and his mother after the wedding. *Sure, Mom,* he'd said. *Paul's great. I'd love it if the two of you got married!* It was only later that he'd discovered his mother's marriage to Paul meant moving more than two hundred miles from the home he and his mother had always shared with his grandparents.

His mother's voice intrudes again. "I've been

seeing signs. For a couple of years, it's been getting more and more obvious. How Leo would ask a question, tell a story, and five minutes later say it all again." She sighs, gazes out the window at the green countryside sliding past. "And the way he left his veterinary practice, just walking out like that . . ."

"I know," Paul says, his deep voice vibrating sympathy. "I know."

Leave my grandfather alone! The words echo in Tim's skull as though someone is inside there shouting them, but no one can hear except him.

His mother certainly doesn't hear. "That time when Sophie called to say he'd gone out into the garden and pulled up all his tomato plants, I knew for sure. He loved his garden so much, tended it so carefully. How could he have done such a thing?"

Paul reaches over to rub the back of Mom's neck. Her neck looks fragile under that big hand, like a twig that could be snapped. But then everything looks small, feels small around Paul.

"What did she do?" Paul asks now, as though he hasn't heard the story before. Maybe Mom's the one with Alzheimer's, repeating herself the way she does.

"Oh, you know Sophie. She gave him a good

scolding. As though she could bring him back that way." Mom lets out a small hiccuping laugh, but the sound is closer to tears.

Tim crosses his arms over his chest and glares at the back of his mother's head. What reason does she have to cry? She's the one who chose to go off and leave Granddad. Besides, he isn't her father. Not even her father-in-law anymore.

Years ago, more than eleven years ago, a young man named Franklin brought his pregnant young wife to his parents' home for the first time. Showed up at their door after years of absence, sat at their table, eating, laughing, telling stories. Then he'd stood up, stretched, and said, casually, "I've got a little errand to run." And off he went, leaving Tim's mother behind. Off he went, never to return.

Tim not even born, his mother young and scared. How often she talks about that. How Grandma and Granddad took her in when she was barely more than a girl. A scared girl about to have a baby.

Not just took her in, either, but made a home for her after her own parents had disowned her for marrying Franklin. And then when Tim was born, they'd made a home for him, too. Until Paul came and took them both away.

Now he and his mother are returning, scared in a whole different way. Tim has been begging to come back ever since they left three months ago. He'd begged not to be taken away from Sheldon, too.

"I'll just stay with Granddad for the summer," he'd said. "Then the two of you can get settled." He figured his mother and Paul would get used to not having him around after a while.

They had a million excuses, though. "You've got to get settled into your new home, too," they'd say. "Begin to make friends . . . get ready for school." Then they'd smile and add, "Besides, we'd miss you too much. You know that."

Nobody stopped to consider, even for a moment, how much his grandfather might miss him.

"I don't know what I'm going to do without you, Timothy," Granddad had said at least a million times. "I don't know what I'll do."

But no one was listening except Tim. And what could an eleven-year-old kid do?

"Sophie's got some hard decisions coming up," Mom says now. "Really hard. But if she—"

"No!"

Tim's mother turns around from the front seat,

her forehead creased beneath her soft, caramel-colored bangs. Brown eyes with golden flecks, but the gold goes into hiding when she's sad. "Tim, you must understand. Your grandfather is—"

"No," he says again. Only that. And he turns his face stubbornly to the window, blocking out the rest of what she says.

Black and white cows munch on green grass. Summer lingers in the bright grass, but the pastures are edged with the vivid red of sumac. The tops of a few of the trees have colored, lit like candles. *Burnt sienna* that color is called in his crayon box.

No, he says once more, but this time only inside his head. And soon *No*, too, becomes part of the hum of the tires. *No, no, no.*

Another pasture. More cows. The cows are Holsteins. Dairy farmers raise cows. Beef farmers raise cattle. He doesn't know why one says "cows," the other says "cattle." Granddad would know. Granddad was a veterinarian, and he knows just about everything. Granddad *is* a veterinarian. He still is, isn't he, even though his clinic has been sold?

Mom goes on talking, talking. Explaining. But Tim doesn't listen. He doesn't need to listen. He knows what he knows.

There is a difference between *sick* and *sad*. His grandfather is sad. First he was sad about Franklin, the son who went away and never came back. Maybe other people didn't know, because he never said it. Nobody in that house ever actually said anything about Franklin. But as long as Tim could remember, he'd seen the Franklin sadness in his grandfather's eyes.

And now Tim has gone away and left him, too.

When Tim was a little baby, Granddad was the one who stayed up with him at night when he had colic. Mom had told him so. "Go to sleep," Granddad would say to Mom. "A new mother needs her sleep." And then he would take Tim downstairs and walk him back and forth, back and forth until Tim slept and finally Granddad could sleep, too.

And wasn't it Granddad who ran alongside Tim's two-wheeler while he wobbled down the middle of the street? Wasn't it Granddad who always knew exactly the right moment to let go?

And Granddad who took him camping, Granddad who taught him about catching fish, cleaning them, frying them in a cast-iron skillet over the camp fire?

Tim loves his mother, of course, and he likes Paul just fine. He's even beginning to think

Minneapolis is okay. But his grandfather? He *owes* his grandfather.

And now, it's payback time.

With Tim home, Granddad will get better. Everyone will see how much better he'll be with Tim there.

And then they'll have no choice.

They'll have to agree that Tim must stay.

TWO

Waiting for the Leaves to Fall

When they step out of the car, Tim sees Granddad first. He is standing in the front doorway, his face glowing like a friendly jack-o'-lantern.

"Here he is!" Granddad calls. He is looking only at Tim. "Here's my boy!"

Tim runs up the porch steps and throws his arms around his grandfather. Granddad isn't big like Paul, but he is solid. He is there. He has not changed.

"Oh, Leo," Mom says when she arrives, "we missed you. I'm sorry it's been so long. It just seemed to take forever to get settled." She pecks him on the cheek.

It's a lie, of course. They were "settled" within a week. Two at the most.

Tim steps back from his grandfather's embrace, ready to contradict his mother, but Granddad winks at him and draws him close again. Tim lets himself be pulled into the rough wool shirt. The shirt smells of fabric softener, but it also carries the tang of the crisp outdoor air and a faint memory of horses. Tim sighs and wraps his arms around his grandfather once more, squeezing with all his might.

Grandma arrives at the door, too. Her hands fluttering. Her hands are like birds looking for a place to land. "Oh, my," she is saying. "Oh, my. Here you are at last. Such a long trip. You must be exhausted." And then with that mock crossness she always uses to cover strong feelings, "For heaven's sake, Leo! Where are your manners? Invite them in!"

"Come in," Granddad booms obediently. "Come in!" He holds the door open, and they all troop inside.

Once in the living room, they stop, facing one another. Everyone is talking at once. Except Tim. Except Granddad. They just stand there on the edge of the small crowd, smiling at each other.

Granddad runs a hand down Tim's sleeve as though to test if there is truly a boy inside. "How's your new school?" he asks.

Tim shrugs. "It's okay. Not as good as Sheldon Elementary, though. Nothing's as good in Minneapolis as here."

11

Granddad's smile widens to a grin. That must have been the answer he was hoping for.

The others go on talking, their voices rising, treading on the ends of one another's sentences.

"Coffee!" Grandma cries above the din. "You need coffee." Strong, fragrant coffee is Grandma's answer for every celebration or woe, weddings, funerals, homecomings. She offers it only to the adults, though. Sometimes, when Grandma and Mom weren't around, Granddad used to give Tim a cup of Grandma's coffee, with lots of cream and two heaping spoonfuls of sugar. Drinking it was like drinking rich, bitter candy.

Grandma always said coffee would stunt Tim's growth. Granddad just said, "Here, boy. This will grow hair on your chest."

Before he was old enough to understand the joke, Tim used to check his chest afterward to see if he had begun to sprout hair.

The others move toward the kitchen, still talking all at once. They leave Granddad and Tim alone in the suddenly quiet living room, leaning into one another in that comfortable, comforting way.

"Well," Granddad says. "Well." And he straightens up, smoothing back his hair and tugging on the front of his wool plaid shirt as though righting himself after an encounter with a strong wind.

Tim pulls himself up straight, too. He smoothes his own hair, tugs on his sweatshirt. "What do you want to do?" he asks. As long as he can remember, he and Granddad have gone off together on "adventures." That's what Granddad calls them, even when the adventure is no more than a walk to Swenson's Drug Store on Walnut Street for an ice-cream cone. Now that Tim is back, they can have a new adventure every day.

Granddad tips his head to one side, clearly weighing the possibilities.

Voices float back from the kitchen.

"How is he?"

"How are you coping, Sophie? It must be so hard!"

"Don't worry. We're here now. You aren't alone anymore."

Alone? Anger rushes through Tim's veins. As though being with Granddad is the same as being alone!

He checks out Granddad's face and sees that he has heard it all, understood it all, too, though they claim he doesn't understand anymore. His smile has faded. His eyes, always such a bright blue that looking into them is like looking into a sunny sky, have grown opaque.

Tim takes his grandfather's hand protectively, but the larger hand doesn't close around his. Instead, Granddad stands for a moment, swaying slightly, then turns abruptly and moves toward the front door.

"Granddad," Tim calls.

Granddad stops, one hand on the doorknob, but he doesn't turn back to Tim. He just stands there, his head lowered.

Tim can't think of anything to say. *I'm sorry? I'm sorry they're treating you like a little kid who doesn't understand anything at all.* He says instead, "Don't you want to do something?"

No answer. Granddad just opens the door, steps out onto the porch and pulls the door shut behind him with a soft click.

Left alone in the living room, Tim bites his lower lip to stop its sudden trembling. He's not going to stand here and bawl. Granddad is upset, that's all. He has a right to be upset.

Paul emerges from the kitchen. "Where'd your grandpa go?" he asks.

Tim shrugs. *How should I know?* the shrug replies, almost insolently. He doesn't trust himself to speak.

Paul glances past Tim to the front window and seems to understand. Sometimes Paul is too good at understanding. He drops one of his huge hands on Tim's shoulder. "You know, don't you, Timothy? Your grandfather isn't himself these days. There were problems before, little problems we all saw, but they're getting pretty bad now."

Up until Paul came along, Granddad was the only person in the world who called Tim *Timothy*. His mother—and Grandma, too—calls him *Timmy* still, though he's long since outgrown such a baby name. *Timothy* is miles from *Timmy*. The name sounds better when his grandfather says it, though.

He ducks out from under the weight of Paul's hand. "What do you expect when you all go off and talk about him that way? He's not deaf, you know."

Paul nods. "I know," he says quietly. And then, as though it will change anything, "I'm sorry."

Tim says nothing. What is there to say? It's his grandfather they should be apologizing to.

Paul shoves his hands into the pockets of his jeans, shifts from foot to foot. "Do you want to do something?" he asks finally. "Go for a walk, maybe? We were stuffed into that car for so long, some fresh air would feel good."

Tim shakes his head. *Not with you*, the shake says, and he figures that Paul gets that message, too, because he doesn't say anything more. He just touches Tim's shoulder again, then quickly withdraws his hand before Tim can pull away. He heads back to the kitchen, where Mom and Grandma are still gabbling at each other.

"Did you see the Buick?" Grandma is saying. "Scraped all along the side. And he doesn't even remember what happened. Or he won't admit it if he does."

"It could have been a person he hit this time," Mom is saying. "It could have been a child."

Tim wonders why, when people want to emphasize how bad something is, they always talk about children being hurt. Are children more important than adults? If they are, why doesn't *he* feel important?

He turns his back on the kitchen voices, stepping to the large picture window. Granddad has taken up a rake and is scratching at the grass, lifting the rake and letting it fall, then pulling it toward himself with short, fierce strokes. At his feet is a small pile of bright leaves from the maple tree that dominates the front yard. A very small pile. It is much too early for raking.

"He gets up in the night," Grandma is saying,

her voice tight with indignation. "Comes down here to the kitchen and turns on the stove. He thinks he's going to cook himself something. You know the man never learned how to boil an egg, but now . . ."

"He could burn himself," Mom murmurs.

"He could burn me up in my bed," Grandma says. She sounds as though she thinks he's trying to do exactly that.

Tim grimaces. He knows it's just his grandmother's way, to sound cross when she's upset. He knows, too, that she loves his grandfather, though her tongue would probably turn to stone before she would say it. But if Granddad really is changing, why can't she change, too? Be less critical. Gentler.

Tim stands there at the window, waiting for Granddad to look up and see him, to motion him to come outside. But he only keeps on with that useless raking, and finally Tim heads for the stairs instead. He runs up both flights so that by the time he reaches the attic he is puffing. Stopping in the doorway, he scans his room. At least that has not changed . . . except for the fact that the bookcase is empty, that there is no mess of toys scattered across the floor. And Grandma has put his old Winnie-the-Pooh bedspread back on the bed, the one he used when he was a little kid.

He loves this room. When he was seven, he'd asked to have it for his own. The house is big, and the bedroom he'd had before, the one next to his mother's on the second floor, is bigger than this one. There was no reason, Grandma and Mom told him over and over again, for him to be in the attic. No reason at all. Except, of course, that this is the best room in the house.

He loves the way the ceiling slopes right down to the floor. The way the windows stand in their own special little alcoves. The way, when the wind blows, one branch of the maple scratches at the roof, like the tree is bending close, talking just to him.

Especially, he loves knowing that this room once belonged to Franklin, once belonged to his father.

"Your grandma fussed about Franklin's wanting to sleep up here, too," Granddad whispered in the midst of all the commotion the two women made. "But it's all right. Sometimes a boy needs his own space."

Tim pushes open a window and peers into the tree. The upper leaves are so brightly colored they seem to be manufacturing their own sunlight. He stretches to see if he can grab the

18

branch that extends over the roof. He can almost reach, but not quite. When his arms are long enough, he's going to catch that branch and swing out into the tree. Then he'll climb down the trunk and walk back in the front door and give everyone a surprise. Just like Franklin used to do.

Granddad will love that!

A chickadee scolds from deep inside the tree. Grandma taught him about birds, so though he can't see it, he knows that's what it is. But beneath and around the "dee-dee-dee" is another sound, the steady scratching of the rake. His grandfather is still down there, tugging at the few leaves scattered in the grass.

A wave of heat suddenly prickles Tim's scalp. What is his grandfather doing, anyway? Trying to give those people in the kitchen something more to talk about?

He leans on the sill. From up here, Granddad looks small, hunched. His silvery hair, always combed straight back neatly without a part, lifts in the breeze and floats about his head like cobwebs. Granddad's hair isn't white because he's old. It's been white for as long as Tim can remember. "Prematurely gray" is what people call it. Prematurely gray, prematurely . . .

"Hey!" Tim calls. "Hey . . . Granddad."

His grandfather looks up. "Hey, yourself," he replies. "What are you doing inside on such a beautiful day?"

"What are you doing out there?"

Granddad looks down at the rake. "Not much," he says. "Not much at all. Just waiting for the leaves to fall." And then he laughs.

See! Tim's heart sings. *The raking is just an excuse to get away from those people.* He joins in the laughter.

"I'll be right down," he calls. "Just wait for me there, Granddad. I'm coming."

THREE

A Plan

When Tim arrives in the front yard, Granddad is still leaning on the rake, still peering up into the red and gold branches of the maple. It is only mid-September, but this tree has always turned ahead of the others in the neighborhood.

"Every autumn I tell this lady not to be in such a hurry," Granddad comments, "but she won't listen. She's too busy thinking about winter to care what an old man says."

"You're not old," Tim objects.

"Ah," his grandfather says. Only that. He reaches down to pick up a bright leaf and twirls it on its vivid red stem. "Maybe she's right. Maybe we are going to have an early winter. . . ." His voice trails off.

Tim shifts uncomfortably from foot to foot. His grandfather isn't talking about the tree any longer, though what he is really talking about, Tim doesn't care to guess.

"Granddad," he says, keeping his voice light, "let's go some place. Just you and me. The way we used to do."

His grandfather squints at him. He seems to be trying to make Tim out from a great distance. "But . . ." He nods toward the house. "Sophie . . ."

"Oh, we won't be gone long. Grandma won't even have time to miss us. Besides, they're all happy as clams in there." *Happy as clams talking about you*, he adds, only to himself.

"Happy as clams?" It is as though Granddad has never heard the expression before, though it's one Grandma uses all the time, and the bemused look on his face causes Tim to wonder, *What's so happy about clams, anyway?*

"Well?" he says. "What do you say?"

But his grandfather doesn't say anything. He just stands there, gazing off toward the house as though he expects Grandma to step out onto the porch and scold him for thinking about leaving the yard.

Finally, Tim takes his hand, dry and slightly cool in that familiar way, and tugs. "Come on," he says softly. "It's been a long time since we've been on an adventure. Do you have your wallet with you? Let's go downtown and get an ice-cream cone at Swenson's Drugs."

"Ice cream?" The words seem to bring his grandfather awake. Ice cream is his favorite food. He's often said it's the only thing he likes better than Grandma's oven-fried chicken and scalloped potatoes. He reaches back to pat the bulge his wallet makes in his back pocket. "I want butter pecan. How about you?"

"You know what I want," Tim reminds him. His grandfather's favorite flavor changes—one week butter pecan, the next orange sherbet or even bubble gum—but Tim's is always the same. He holds his breath. Surely Granddad will remember.

"One scoop of chocolate. One of peppermint. With the peppermint on top." Granddad grins triumphantly. He is right and he knows it.

Tim releases his breath, grins back. "You've got it," he says, and they start toward the front walk.

When they reach the edge of his grandparents' property, Tim glances back over his shoulder toward the house. No one is visible through the living room window. No one to see them going and to object. Apparently, his mother and Paul and his grandmother are still in the kitchen, complaining about Granddad.

Tim squares his shoulders. This is what Granddad needs, a little time alone with his grandson. Once he knows that Tim is home, really home to stay, everything will be all right again.

At the corner of Walnut and Third, Granddad comes to a full stop on the curb in front of the hardware store.

"Swenson's is this way," Tim reminds him, nodding in the direction of the drug store, though, of course, his grandfather knows perfectly well where it is. The main street of Sheldon isn't long. Tim can see to each end from where they stand.

But Granddad doesn't seem to hear. He just stands there, shuffling his feet as though he can't make up his mind which way to go. A breeze picks up a few dry leaves and sends them spinning along the gutter.

When he finally speaks, his voice is low. "She wants to get rid of me, you know." He gazes off down the street as though he is talking about someone he sees in the distance. "She's been trying to get rid of me for a long time now."

"Who?" Tim looks down the empty street, too, then up at his grandfather. Who could he be talking about?

"Sophie. She wants to put me away."

Grandma? Put him away? That makes no sense!

"She's got the place all picked out. The one where she's going to put me."

Tim frowns. He doesn't like listening to this. It sounds . . . well, the truth is, it sounds crazy. Since his grandfather doesn't seem to be about to move either up the street or down, Tim leads him to the rickety bench in front of the hardware store. "What place does she have picked out?" he asks. "What do you mean?"

The bench creaks as they sit. But Tim hears even more clearly the sound of the condescension in his own voice. It makes him swallow hard. There is a tone adults use when they are humoring children, and he has just spoken to his grandfather that way.

"It's one of those places"—Granddad speaks slowly and distinctly, as if to someone who is having difficulty understanding English—"the kind where they send old people to die. Especially old people who've lost their marbles."

The kind where they send old people to die? Especially old people who've lost their marbles? Granddad must be talking about a nursing home! If his tongue had been jerked out, Tim couldn't have been left more speechless.

Granddad's angry glare seems to be meant for

Tim, too. "She's got no use for this old plow horse any longer, so she's putting me out to pasture. Only I don't much like the pasture she's got in mind."

"But Grandma would never put you in a nursing home," Tim protests finally. "I know she wouldn't."

Granddad snorts. "Don't be so sure. I've heard. I've heard her talking on the phone to your mother. She's going to sell the house. Then she'll have 'enough money,' she says." His voice rises to a falsetto imitation of Grandma's when he says "enough money."

"That's why your mother's come back . . . to help Sophie get the house ready to sell. 'Sharper than a serpent's tooth . . .'"

He doesn't finish, but Tim knows the rest of the quote. He's heard his grandmother use it before, though never about his mother. *How sharper than a serpent's tooth it is to have a thankless child.*

"No!" he cries. Just as he had cried to his mother earlier. What had she been talking about then? A nursing home? Is that what all the explaining had been about? He should have listened.

He had been so sure that he was going to come

back here and fix everything that he hadn't seen any need to pay attention to what the adults were planning.

But sell the house? His grandfather's house? His father's house. His! Sell the house and shut Granddad away in a nursing home?

Tim knows about nursing homes. There isn't one in Sheldon, but Beckwith, the next town to the east, has one. He's been inside it, even. The Sunday school kids from the Lutheran church used to sing carols over there at Christmas every year. People are always talking about how "nice" the Beckwith nursing home is. And maybe it does have pretty wallpaper. Polished floors. Nurses who wear pastel colors instead of that institutional white.

But the whole place is filled with old people. *Really* old! The kind of old people who sit hunched over in wheelchairs or shuffle along the corridors with walkers. The kind of old people who look at you and don't even seem to know you're there.

Granddad in a nursing home? No way. Not in a thousand, million years.

But what could he do? What could any kid do?

Him and his dumb plan. Here he'd thought all he had to do was to come back and stay with his grandfather, get him kind of plumped up, like a pillow that requires a good shake and a few pats to be right again.

But he should have realized the adults would be making plans, too.

"Granddad," Tim says, and this time his words come out settled, certain. "I have an idea. A better idea than going for ice cream. I know exactly the kind of adventure we need."

Granddad waits, his head inclined to one side.

Tim is so filled with pride—his grandfather is depending on him for his very life!—that he has a hard time speaking. "You and me . . . we . . . can run away."

"Run away?" The expectation in Granddad's face slides into confusion. "Where would we go?"

But Tim has the answer to that, too. The absolutely perfect answer. "We'll go camping. Just like we used to do. We'll go out to Silver Lake, go fishing—get us a mess of sunnies, maybe even a walleye or two. We'll eat berries, mushrooms . . . " Tim hates mushrooms, but that doesn't matter. He'll learn to like them. "We'll live off the land." He grips his grandfather's arm. "And we won't come back until we're good and ready. Grandma can't put you in a nursing home if she can't find you!"

28

For a long moment, Granddad stares. Then his mouth starts jerking at the corners, and for a moment Tim thinks, to his horror, that his grandfather is going to cry. But he shakes his head and says, so sweetly, so reasonably that Tim almost wants to cry himself, "That won't help, you know. We'd have to come back sooner or later. And soon as we did, she'd pack me off to that blasted nursing home for sure."

"But don't you see? If you show them you can still take care of yourself—out in the woods, even—they'll have to know you're okay. Someone who can do all that can't possibly belong in a nursing home."

Granddad studies Tim for a long time before a slow smile begins to spread across his face. "Sophie would love to have a good mess of sunnies to fry up," he says.

Tim waits.

"Fishing!" Granddad's eyes shine. "I haven't been fishing for . . . not since before you and your mama went off with that Paul fellow."

Went off with that Paul fellow. Tim can't help but cringe.

But then, as quickly as it came, Granddad's smile fades. "Keys." He plunges his hands into his pants pockets and withdraws them again, empty. "Sophie took my keys to the Buick. She says I'm not to drive anymore."

Not drive! Tim's hope fades like his grandfather's smile. He knew that. It's one of the things Grandma was talking about in the kitchen. And the state forest preserve and the Silver Lake campground is ten, maybe fifteen miles outside of town. Too far to walk, that's for sure. Paul would take them. Paul would take Tim just about anywhere he asks to go. But they can hardly ask Paul to help them run away.

There has to be another answer.

And then it dawns on him. The solution. The absolutely perfect solution.

"The pickup camper," Tim says.

Granddad frowns. "That's gone. She sold that to—"

"Grandma sold it to Dr. Hutchins. Last spring when he bought your practice." Tim speaks quickly, urgently. "But he's an okay guy. If we go by the clinic and ask if we can borrow the camper, just for a little while, he'll let us, I'm sure."

For a long moment Granddad just sits there, kicking at a patch of broken concrete in front of the bench. Tim watches him, wondering if he heard, if he understood.

Finally, though, Granddad straightens his shoulders. The smile he had cut off earlier plumps out his cheeks. "That young whipper-snapper," he says. "Calls himself a vet? Why, I've forgotten more than he ever knew."

"That's for sure, Granddad. That's for sure."

Granddad nods his head, once, twice. "We'll go fishing."

Tim sighs. This plan will work. Once he gets his grandfather away from all that talk about "burning down the house" and "hurting children," he'll be fine. Everyone will have to see that he is fine.

Tim rises from the bench. "Come with me," he says.

Granddad stands, too, and they start toward the veterinary clinic. For the first time since Tim returned to Sheldon, his grandfather's shoulders are back, his head high, his step light.

And the humming racket in Tim's head has turned to pure song.

I'm going to take care of Granddad. Granddad will take care of me. We'll show them. We'll show them all.

FOUR

Gone Fishin'

Granddad bursts into the Sheldon Veterinary Clinic the way Santa must drop down chimneys, full of good cheer and an absolute certainty of his welcome. Seeing him back within these walls makes Tim feel warm all over. Granddad was always most fully himself when he was at the clinic. Why he'd decided to quit his practice and why Grandma had been so ready to sell it, Tim has never understood.

Mrs. Hutchins, Dr. Hutchins's wife, is standing behind the new counter they have installed. The counter makes the place look more formal. The counter and the beautiful young woman standing behind it, too. Mrs. Hutchins is wearing a silky green blouse. *Not exactly the kind of clothes a person wears who is truly going to help out around a veterinary clinic*, Tim can't help but note.

"Dr. Leo! How good to see you," Mrs. Hutchins calls. "And Timmy. You're back in town!" She tosses her head, which causes her tawny mane of hair to swirl and resettle.

Tim nods, though inwardly he can't help but bristle at the *Timmy*. The name is bad enough coming from his mother and his grandmother.

"How are you?" Granddad is saying. "How's business? Have the farmers been having trouble with milk fever lately?" And then, before Mrs. Hutchins can answer any of his questions, "Is your hubby here? Do you suppose Timothy and I could have a word with him?"

"Sure, he's here, Dr. Leo," she says. "But he's with a patient now. Could the two of you wait for a few minutes?"

Granddad looks over at Tim, as though it's up to him to decide.

"Sure." Tim deepens his voice. "We can wait. For a little while, anyway."

Apparently satisfied, Granddad nods and turns to the waiting room.

A rather portly middle-aged man sits in one of the orange plastic chairs holding an equally portly cat. The cat is long haired with a cross-looking, snub-nosed face. She reminds Tim of the principal of his new school.

"Muffins!" Granddad exclaims, addressing the cat.

Tim has heard his grandmother comment that during the last couple of years of his veterinary practice Granddad had increasing difficulty remembering the names of the people he served, but seemed never to forget the name of an animal patient. In fact, she claimed he could walk down the aisle of a milking parlor and name every cow—"Bessie, Milly, Fiona"—but afterward not remember the name of the farmer so he could send out a bill.

Granddad approaches Muffins. In response, the cat narrows her eyes, flattens her ears, and opens her triangular pink mouth in a prolonged hiss.

"Ah-ha!" Granddad exclaims. "She remembers me!"

Everyone laughs.

Granddad reaches out slowly and begins to scratch Muffins's chin, the place along the jaw bone where every cat in the world loves to be scratched.

Muffins accepts the attention, stretching her neck to assist him in reaching exactly the right spot, but when he quits scratching, she hisses again.

Everyone laughs once more.

"Cats are intelligent creatures," Granddad pronounces. "Far more intelligent, I can't help but

believe, than dogs. I know folks assume dogs
have more brains, because a dog can be taught to
obey. But think about it. Does it take more up
here"—he taps his forehead—"to be a leader or
a follower? What do you say, Timothy?"

It was a discussion they'd had before, and Tim
knows how to answer. "It takes more brains to
think for yourself," he says.

Granddad nods, pleased with the response, as
always. "I can tell you about intelligence in a
cat." He seems to be speaking not only to the
man or to Mrs. Hutchins behind the desk or to
Tim but to a room full of people who aren't here.
The people of Sheldon he left behind when he
quit his practice, perhaps. "I knew a fellow who
had a cat. She was female, and as will happen if
no one takes care of the situation, every spring
she had a litter of kittens."

Tim knows the story. It's one Granddad once
read to him from an encyclopedia about cats.
Only he's never before heard him tell it as
though it had happened to someone he knew.

In the story, the cat's owner didn't want the
trouble of finding homes for a litter of four or five
kittens, so when they were born, he drowned all
but one kitten and left that one for the mother
cat to rear. The next spring when the kittens

came again, he did the same thing. The spring after that, the cat became pregnant again, but this time produced only one kitten. The owner was surprised, but relieved. After all, no one likes killing kittens. Then, four or five weeks later three more kittens came out of hiding.

"See," Granddad says, concluding his story, "she left one kitten out for everyone to see, because she knew that one would be safe, and the rest she kept tucked away. Now, don't you think that's smart?"

Mrs. Hutchins and the man agree that was, indeed, smart. Tim agrees, too. Because the story does prove the cat's intelligence, no matter whether it came from a book or from Granddad's own experience.

Dr. Hutchins appears from behind the door of the examining room. "Leo!" he says. "How good to see you. What are you doing here?"

"Just telling old Muffins here a story," Granddad says, and Dr. Hutchins looks confused. Tim notes with satisfaction that young Dr. Hutchins doesn't seem to know who Muffins is. It will be a long time before he will know his practice the way Granddad did.

Granddad nods in Tim's direction. "We came to ask a favor," he explains, "my grandson and me."

Dr. Hutchins smiles. One front tooth overlaps the other crookedly, giving him a slightly nerdy look, but he seems friendly enough.

"That old pickup camper I sold you a while back . . ."

"Yes?" Dr. Hutchins's glance slides cautiously to his wife.

Tim bristles. Why is the man looking at his wife that way? And what does he need her here for, anyway, pretending he's got some kind of big city clinic that requires a receptionist up front to greet the patients? When people brought their pets to see Granddad, they knew when his office hours were and they just came. No one had to greet them, to tell them to sit down and wait.

Tim was the only help Granddad ever had . . . or wanted, and he didn't waste his time standing out front greeting people, either. He did important work like cleaning out the cages and walking the dogs. Sometimes he went out to farms with Granddad, too. He'd even helped deliver a calf once.

"Well, you see," Granddad is explaining, "it was Sophie's idea to sell the thing. Never mine. I'm not such an old man that I—"

Tim interrupts. "We'd like to borrow it. That's

all. Just for a little while. If you don't mind, that is."

"Going fishing, Tim?" Dr. Hutchins asks. Again he checks out his wife in that sneaky way. You'd think the man couldn't do anything without her approval, couldn't even decide whether to loan a lousy secondhand camper back to its real owner or not.

"Yes," Tim says firmly. "We're going fishing."

"Just you and your grandpa?" It's Mrs. Hutchins asking now.

Tim suddenly understands the territory they are in. Grandma has talked to these people. Heaven only knows what she told them about his grandfather when she sold them the clinic and the camper. Now they have it in their heads that he's not to be trusted anymore. Not even with a camper he's repaired, driven, gone camping in for years and years!

"Not just us," Tim says, his words tumbling over one another in his urgency to get them said. "Paul, too. You know Paul Boyce? He married my mother. He's busy right now, so he told Granddad and me to come ask about using the camper. The three of us using it, that is. But Paul's the one going to drive and everything like that."

Tim is not a good liar. Never has been. When

he is through with that jumble of words, his palms are itching with sweat and his face burns.

Granddad looks from Dr. Hutchins to Tim, obviously confused. Tim keeps his fingers crossed, hoping his grandfather won't contradict him.

"Oh well, then," Dr. Hutchins says, "of course. You may certainly borrow the camper. You just tell Paul that it's parked back behind the garage at my house and the key is under the mat on the driver's side. He can come and drive it away."

Tim tries to look casual, as though he had known all along that Dr. Hutchins would lend them the camper. But relief leaves his knees suddenly watery.

"The three of you go and have a good time," Mrs. Hutchins chirps, giving that great mane of hair another toss. "I'm sure that old truck will be glad to be camping again. We've been so busy with the practice, we've hardly had a chance to use it the whole summer long."

"It's kind of you," Granddad is saying. "Truly kind. My grandson here," he puts an arm around Tim's shoulders, "wants to go fishing . . . real bad."

"I do," Tim agrees as he reaches for the handle of the door.

When they emerge together into the September

sunshine, Tim feels like leaping into the air, clicking his heels together, shouting. His plan is going to work. In every way it will work.

"Well, boy," Granddad says, "are you ready for an adventure?" His eyes sparkle like deep water. Like the water where the walleye are waiting.

"I'm ready. I've never been more ready for anything in my whole life! We haven't been fishing since forever." Tim dances a little jig in the middle of the walk.

Granddad stops to watch, his face glowing. When Tim stands still again, his grandfather lifts a hand and traces the contours of his face, running the tips of his fingers down Tim's cheek and, very gently, along his jaw.

Tim leans into the hand, his heart filled to overflowing.

His grandfather speaks softly but distinctly. "It *has* been forever," he says. "Forever and forever. Why did we let it get to be so long, Franklin?"

FIVE

Making Change

It doesn't matter, Tim reminds himself for the hundredth time. It doesn't matter that Granddad called him Franklin. He's made that little mistake hundreds of times before. Thousands of times, probably. And not just since he's been "sick," either. He'd been doing it as far back as Tim can remember. Even Grandma slips and calls him *Franklin* sometimes. Mom's the only one in the family who doesn't do it, but then she never says the name *Franklin* at all. Not if she can help it, anyway.

The camper rattles along the county road that will take them to the state forest preserve and Silver Lake. The road is narrow, with lots of bumpy tar seams and potholes in the concrete, but the seams and the potholes don't matter. Nothing matters but getting to the lake, getting out the fishing poles stowed in the back of the camper, getting Granddad away from these people who are so sure he can't do anything right anymore.

Tim glances over at his grandfather, at the familiar hands, square and competent, resting on the steering wheel. How unfair for Grandma to tell him he can't drive anymore just because of one little accident! There is nothing wrong with Granddad's driving. He drives the way he always has, like a man in charge of his world. He drives like a man who is glad to be taking his one and only grandson camping.

In fact, from the time Tim located the camper parked behind the Hutchins's garage and found the key under the floor mat, Granddad has taken over. He knows exactly what to do, where to go. Just as Tim had been certain he would.

Granddad speaks without taking his eyes from the road. "I used to take your dad fishing at Silver Lake." He says it as though he is beginning one of his stories, but then he goes silent.

Tim isn't surprised when nothing more is forthcoming. He has always been hungry for information about his father, but no one in the family—including his grandfather—has ever been willing to give more than the briefest, most unsatisfactory answers. *No, we don't know where*

Franklin went. We don't know why he went, either. He had problems, that's all.

It was obvious that a man who would abandon his wife and unborn baby had *problems*, but what kind no one would say.

Was he in trouble with the law? Was he sick? Had he gone off somewhere to save his parents and his young wife the pain of seeing him waste away?

Tim used to go through Grandma's old photo album studying the fuzzy-headed baby in Grandma's arms, the little boy with knobby knees grinning from a tricycle, the teenager with his arm around a girl who isn't Tim's mother. He used to stare and stare at those pictures, trying to figure it all out. Who Franklin Palmer was. Why he didn't bother to wait around to meet his own son.

The worst part of not knowing his father is not knowing what to think about him. How to feel. Tim used to know a boy named Billy Pritchard whose dad regularly got drunk and beat up Billy's mom and Billy and his older brother, too. Billy hated his father. He'd say it to just about anybody. "I hate my old man!" And strange as it might seem, sometimes Tim used to envy him that fierce hate. At least Billy felt *something*. A good solid hate would be better than the blank that expands inside Tim's gut every time the subject of Franklin Palmer comes up.

He has tried hating his father. He has tried loving him, too. Either one is like pumping air into a leaky tire. The moment he quits pumping, the tire goes flat.

Today, though, he's not sure he wants the ghost of the boy Franklin standing between him and his grandfather. This trip is too important to include anyone else, even his father.

Tim's stomach gives out a complaining rumble, and he lays a hand across it. He isn't sure what time it is—the clock on the dashboard is broken—but they must have missed lunch by at least an hour. Probably more. "I'm starved," he says. "How about you?"

Granddad shrugs. "I guess we'll have to catch a fish or two," he says. "Cook them over a fire."

That's what Tim had suggested, of course. Just the two of them, living off the land. Still, he is awfully hungry. "We'll have to stop at Melvin's for bait, though. Don't you think? Couldn't we pick up some food there? Just bread and peanut butter. Maybe hot chocolate, too. To tide us over until we can catch some fish." Melvin's is a small gas station, bait shop, and grocery store, the last sign of civilization before they enter the state forest.

"Melvin has that good salami," Granddad says.

"Salami for you," Tim agrees. "Peanut butter and jelly for me." He is not fond of salami, especially the kind Melvin sells . . . heavy with garlic and with little white blobs of fat all through it.

"Salami for you," Granddad repeats. "Peanut butter and jelly for me."

Tim considers correcting him, but there is no need. He's probably just joking, anyway.

For the next few miles they talk about this and that. The time Tim caught a big muskie and was scared so badly by the fish's teeth that, before Granddad could stop him, he had cut the line rather than bring it into the boat. About Brandy, Granddad's lovable old dog, the last in a long line of golden retrievers all bearing the same name. Brandy had died last winter at the grand age of seventeen, and while everyone else was grieving, Grandma had announced, in that no-nonsense way of hers, "I'm not housebreaking another puppy, so don't even think about it."

"I don't know how Sophie can live without a dog around," Granddad says now.

She's mean, Tim thinks. But he knows better than to say it.

Besides, she's never been mean to him. Though how she could come up with the idea of a nursing home is more than he can understand.

"And then," Granddad adds, "she went and gave Marmalade away."

Tim doesn't comment on that. Marmalade was Grandma's orange tabby cat, and Tim was the one she'd given him to. She'd figured the cat would just "fade away" if Tim didn't take him to Minneapolis. That's what she'd said, anyway. The truth was, she'd known how much Tim was going to miss that old cat curled into a purring ball at the foot of his bed.

Tim shifts in his seat. He wishes his mother had let him bring Marmalade back with him instead of leaving him with a neighbor. Now they were going to be separated for sure.

They are approaching a turn onto a narrow gravel road. The road runs across an open meadow until it disappears into the shadow of the dense forest. A ramshackle frame building with a faded sign proclaiming MELVIN'S stands at the corner. Granddad makes the turn into the parking lot in a single sharp movement so that the back wheels fishtail a bit when the vehicle hits the gravel.

They sit side by side, waiting for the plume of their dust to drift away from the camper. The store looks deserted, but then Tim can't remember a time when it didn't. Granddad has always referred to Melvin's as a not-for-profit store, existing, as far as anyone could tell, merely to give Melvin an excuse to live alone here at the edge of the woods.

Tim steps out of the camper, sniffing the air, so different from the air in the city. Different, even, from the air in Sheldon. Plants. Good, clean dirt! He can almost smell the lake, too, though they will have to follow the gravel road for two or three more miles before they reach its closest shore.

Granddad climbs out on the other side of the camper and gives a long, lazy stretch. "What did we want at Melvin's?" he asks finally, peering over the roof of the camper at Tim.

"Bait," Tim reminds him. "We need minnows. And bread and peanut butter, too." He doesn't mention the salami. Even if he doesn't have to eat it, he has to put up with Granddad's garlic breath after he does.

"Ah, yes." Granddad winks. "Just checking to see if you remembered."

Tim winks back. Grandma would have scolded Granddad. She would have tried to make him admit that he had forgotten, yet again. He's heard her do it a million times. But he's not going to be like that.

Inside, the store smells of raw meat, wooden floors, and another smell, lush and comforting, that always reminds Tim of summer rain. That's the bait tanks. Granddad has brought the bait bucket from the back of the camper, and he heads for the minnows. The sign says CRAPPIES, $2.50 A SCOOP.

Tim goes in search of the peanut butter and a loaf of bread. Melvin's carries Wonder Bread, he remembers. Grandma bakes her own bread, and she won't allow Wonder Bread in her house. She calls it "baked air." And considering that you can take a slice and roll it into a ball no bigger than a marble, the name is apt. She doesn't understand, though. Just because she makes great homemade bread doesn't mean a person can't love Wonder Bread as well. Tim even likes the way it flattens out and sticks to the roof of his mouth when he eats it. He finds some cocoa, too, and a small jar of grape jelly.

He sets his purchases down on the counter in front of Granddad, who is discussing the weather with Melvin. Granddad looks over the choices he has made, then picks up the jar of peanut butter. "Mouse bait," he says.

Melvin pushes up the front of his shirt to scratch his round, hairy belly. He nods, his eyes half closed. Does he recognize the story that's coming?

"Granddad—" Tim cuts in, but his grandfather has already begun.

"When I was a young man, I spent a summer working in a fishery in Alaska. And was that work! Standing on the slime line hour after hour, slitting open fish, scooping them out." He gives an exaggerated shudder. "But even worse than standing up to your elbows in fish guts, worse than the occasional grizzly we met walking back to our quarters, were the mice. They took over the shacks where we lived. They ran across our faces when we slept. One of them even ran up inside my pants leg one evening when I was sitting on the edge of my bunk, reading."

Tim has definitely heard the story before. He heads back into the aisles of groceries, Granddad's voice trailing after him.

"The other fellows I worked with devised a trap. You take a bucket, see, and you fill it half full of water—"

Melvin interrupts. "That will be seven dollars, even."

"You fill it half full of water," Granddad repeats, increasing his volume. "Then you put a string across the top, and you put the string through a cardboard roll. The kind left over from toilet paper or paper towels, you know?"

"Seven dollars," Melvin says again. His voice is flat, bored.

Who cares if the man knows the story? He doesn't have to be rude. Tim finds himself standing in front of the meat counter, in front of the salami.

Granddad raises his volume another notch, still ignoring the interruption. "You slather the roll with peanut butter, see? And you lean a board up against the bucket. Then you go to bed."

Tim picks up a package of salami. Is it possible he can smell the garlic? Even through the plastic?

He's never liked this story himself. You go to bed, and all through the night you hear, scrabble, scrabble, scrabble . . . splash. Because the silly mice run up the board and out onto the peanut butter–covered roll, which of course, spins around and dumps them into the half-filled bucket. One mouse after another falls into the water, then they swim and swim and swim until they are too tired to swim any longer. When they can't swim another stroke, when they can't lift their trembling whiskers above the water, when they no longer care about the smell of peanut butter overhead, they drown. One mouse after another drowns.

"When you get up in the morning," Granddad concludes, "you've got a bucket of dead mice to throw out."

Tim studies the label on the salami. He shouldn't be worrying about dead mice. He has told everybody, his mother, his grandmother, most importantly Granddad, that he is going to be a vet one day, and veterinarians have to be tough. To help animals, there are times when you have to hurt them. Like giving shots. Like cutting them open for surgery. Sometimes you even have to "put them down." Which is just a nice way of saying you have to kill them. Though he can't help but wonder if he'll ever be able to do that. However good the cause.

Mice are a nuisance, of course. Everybody says so. No one is supposed to care if they die. But he's never been able to see why. Dead is dead. And a mouse must be as glad to be alive as any other creature.

Tim brings the package of salami and slaps it down on the counter next to the bag Melvin has filled. Granddad is stuffing some bills back into his pocket. Tim is glad the story is done. Melvin must be glad, too, though he doesn't look it. But then he never looks glad about anything, not even customers.

Melvin picks up the salami, arches a grizzled eyebrow at Granddad.

"Sure," Granddad says. "Sure. The boy loves salami."

"You're the one who loves salami, Granddad. Don't you remember?" Tim can hear the impatience in his voice, though he doesn't know why he's feeling impatient, exactly.

"Two thirty-seven," Melvin says.

Granddad reaches back into his pocket, comes out with two dollar bills and some change, hands the bills to Melvin. Then he stirs the change in his hand, his forehead crinkling as though he has no idea how to pick out thirty-seven cents.

Melvin scratches his belly again. His fingernails rasp against his hairy skin.

Granddad keeps stirring. "Here," he says at last, and he thrusts his hand, containing the entire pile of change, toward Melvin. "Take what you need." His face is red, and Tim's own cheeks heat up, too. It's one thing for Granddad to forget that his grandson doesn't like salami. Is it possible to forget how to count change?

The idea settles in the bottom of Tim's stomach like a stone. Could the grownups be right about his grandfather? Is he really "losing it"?

Melvin grunts, takes the appropriate coins from Granddad's palm, and drops them into his change drawer. Without a word, Granddad stuffs the rest into his pocket and heads for the door. Tim picks up the bait bucket and the bag of groceries and follows.

"Hope you have good fishing," Melvin calls after them unexpectedly.

Granddad, always friendly, always ready to carry on a cheerful conversation, pushes out the door without replying.

"Thanks," Tim mumbles. Halfway to the door, he even turns back as though there might be more to say. Like maybe, *Would you like to come with us?*

But that's silly. Of course. He doesn't even like Melvin.

Besides, this is Tim's special time with his grandfather. The two of them are running away together. Why would he want to have Melvin along?

SIX

Something to Prove

Tim stands over the plastic foot pump, pressing it again and again, watching the inflatable raft come slowly to life with each puff of air. *Change!* the pump huffs with each breath. *Change. Granddad can't even make change.*

Tim stops pumping. It's a stupid thought. Just because Granddad let Melvin make change for him is no proof he can't do it himself. And even if he *has* forgotten a little thing like that, it's hardly worth worrying about. Hardly worth any more worry than a bucket of dead mice.

Dead mice, says the pump when he starts up again. *Change.*

Stop! Tim commands his brain. *Just stop!* He steps away from the pump and gives himself a shake.

Why does he have to go spoiling everything? He's here at Silver Lake with his grandfather. They are going to go fishing. Isn't that exactly what he wanted?

The day is crisp and clear with an occasional woolly cloud grazing across the sky. The lake is calm, the breeze just cool enough for the sweat-shirt he is wearing to feel good. And Granddad drove right to their favorite camping spot without hesitating once. Not bad for a man people claim has this thing called Alzheimer's disease.

Granddad had remembered where the inflat-able raft was stored, too, folded away in the spe-cial compartment he'd built on the back of the camper to hold it. And he'd gone right to his fish-ing gear in its battered old box.

Grandma should have seen how happy he was to lay his hands on that gear. Maybe that would make her think twice about selling anything else of Granddad's.

Tim resumes pumping, the air shushing into the raft in sharp bursts.

They'll catch a mess of sunnies and fry them in the black cast-iron skillet over the campfire . . . or a filet from a nice fat walleye. He'll gather acorns, too. There are a lot of those around. The Indians used to make flour from the acorns. Maybe they could have acorn-flour pancakes with their fish.

Granddad emerges from the back of the camper and hands Tim a sandwich. Peanut butter and jelly, the dark purple jelly already oozing through the soft bread, just the way he likes it.

Tim takes a big bite. "Grandma never should have sold the camper," he says around the wad of bread and peanut butter. "That was a dumb thing to do."

The words just pop out, impossible to retrieve once they're said, and Tim quits chewing, waiting for the inevitable response. Granddad has never permitted him to criticize his grandmother. In fact, saying something bad about Grandma has always been the quickest way to bring down his wrath.

This time, though, Granddad only grimaces and says, "I suppose she's afraid if we men go off together, we'll have too much fun."

Tim smiles at that—*we men!*—and begins to chew once more.

After a few more bites of the sandwich he realizes how thirsty he is. And remembers, too, that they didn't buy any pop or juice. They didn't even remember to take on water for the camper's holding tank, so he can't get a drink from the sink inside the camper or make up some cocoa. And the pumps in the campground are always turned off after Labor Day to avoid frozen pipes.

Well, they'll just have to drive back to Melvin's

later and get water. This time the forgetting was his fault as much as Granddad's. The two of them are out of practice, that's all. It's been too long since they've had a chance to go camping.

Granddad gets out the tackle box and begins riffling through it.

"I think we'll use lures," he says, though the bucket of minnows is at his feet. "We can jig." Jigging, in this case, isn't a dance. It's a way of tugging on the line to keep a lure moving.

Tim doesn't reply. He doesn't mind fishing with a lure if that's what Granddad wants.

Granddad studies the lake and, after a long moment, takes out an orange and chartreuse lure and a lead head. Tim thinks the head he is using is the one called a "modified round," but he's not sure.

The camper had been sold in the spring, and he and his grandfather hadn't gone fishing even once before he and Mom moved this past summer. But the summer and fall before, Granddad had taught him which color lure to use, which head style, which weight for different conditions.

For jigging, one color lure is better for early morning, another for clear water on a bright day, another for murky water, another for a cloudy day or for evening. Tim tries to remember what kind of light conditions orange and chartreuse are good for, but he has forgotten. Granddad has so much to teach him still. He remembers about the modified round head, though. That is the best shape for avoiding snags.

People who don't fish—like his mom and his grandmother—think fishing is a simple activity. They think fishermen just go out in a boat and drop a line into the water and they catch fish or they don't and that's all there is to it. But it's not that way at all. Being a good fisherman requires knowledge and respect. You have to *know* the fish you're going after the way you know your best friend. Granddad always says that. You have to know and respect the creature you are going after. It's not just food you're taking; it's life itself. The fish's life to sustain yours.

His grandfather respects every kind of life . . . except, perhaps, for mice. Tim shakes his head— why is he thinking about mice?—and pumps harder.

When the floor of the raft, the last section to be done, is full and tight, Tim joins his grandfather on the picnic bench. "Did you have a sandwich, too?" he asks.

"Sure," Granddad replies. But then he adds in apparent contradiction, "I wasn't hungry."

Tim wonders which it was. Did he have a sandwich or wasn't he hungry enough to want to eat? Maybe he wasn't hungry, but he had a sandwich anyway. He decides not to push the subject.

Granddad's fingers, usually so swift to assemble weight and lure, keep tangling in the line. "Piffle!" he says finally.

It's a private joke between them. Once, when Granddad caught Tim using a bad word, he'd said, "Don't you mean piffle?" And from that point on, piffle has become their favorite "swear word." Once Tim forgot and said it at school and everyone laughed. He's come to rather like the sound of it, though.

"We could tightline," he suggests. Even he can set up for tightlining. Nothing needed except a hook for the minnow and a weight, set about a foot up the line.

Granddad doesn't reply. He just thrusts the entire mess into Tim's hands, stands and heads for the outhouse, moving briskly.

Tim watches his grandfather's retreat for a moment, uncertain how to react. Granddad has never left him to set up the lines on his own. He has always been meticulous about such things, wanting the lines, the weights, the lures to be exactly right. In fact, Tim has sometimes grown impatient with the constant demonstrations, the endless explanations, wanting just to tie the knot himself or choose a lure because he likes its color or its shape, instead of because it's the one Granddad says is right for the conditions.

So apparently his grandfather thinks he's ready. At last!

Smiling to himself, Tim gets the jackknife out of the tackle box. He cuts away the mess of tangled line, drops the lure back into the box, and starts over again with a simple hook and weight. By the time his grandfather is back, he has both poles set up. He sits holding them, waiting for Granddad to come over to check them out, but he doesn't even do that. He just busies himself locking the camper.

Tim isn't sure whether to be pleased or disappointed. Is his grandfather so sure of him that he doesn't even think his work needs checking? Or doesn't he care what Tim has done?

Tim puts the poles in the raft, drags it down to the water, and sets it afloat.

"Come on, Granddad," he calls. "Old Marble Eyes is waiting." *Old Marble Eyes* is what his grandfather calls the walleye.

Tim climbs in, holding the raft close to the shore with one oar.

His grandfather approaches, but stops a few feet away. "Do you think Sophie is going to be cross?" he asks. His voice is plaintive. Almost childlike.

"Who cares if she is?" Tim replies, more firmly than he feels. Though his grandmother blusters a lot, she is seldom genuinely angry. When she does get angry, though, she is a force to be reckoned with. And there is no question, she will be angry this time. Since she's decided that Granddad has "lost his marbles," she will probably direct most of her wrath at Tim. Maybe that's only fair, though. Running away was his idea. "We'll go back when we're good and ready," he adds. "We've got something to prove, remember?"

"What have we got to prove?" his grandfather asks, still from the shore.

"That you don't belong in a nursing home," Tim reminds him. "That you can take care of yourself."

"I can." Granddad straightens his back.

"Yes," Tim agrees. "You can. Now, why don't you come get in and we'll go catch us some supper? I don't want peanut butter and jelly again. And I don't want your stinky salami, either."

Granddad grins. "Best salami in the world. Nice and garlicky. Excellent fat."

It's an argument they've played out many times before, and Tim laughs.

His grandfather rolls up his pants legs, and then, still grinning, wades into the lake. He just steps right in and walks toward the side of the raft.

The only problem is that he hasn't thought to remove his shoes and socks. He's wearing good leather shoes.

Tim had opened his mouth to speak, to try to stop him before he stepped into the water, but there wasn't time. Now there is nothing to be done but to watch him come. Watch him sit on the side of the raft, pushing the inflated edge down so far that Tim expects the boat to start taking on water. Then, just before the water can begin pour in, he tips over backwards. Just topples into the raft, landing on his back on the soft floor, his dripping shoes waving in the air.

Grandma will have a fit about those shoes.

Tim stares at his grandfather. He has always been a dignified man. Loving, funny, helpful, but slightly formal. Not the kind to get down on the floor to play games. And here he is, lying on his back in the bottom of the raft, arms and legs sticking up, giggling. The very sight of him, looking like an overturned turtle, is a shock, and all around them, the world seems shocked, too. Even the birds and the buzzing flies go silent.

But then a squirrel scolds from a nearby tree, a red-winged blackbird in a stand of cattails nearby resumes his lilting song, and Tim reaches to give his grandfather a hand.

"Here, let me help you," he says, and he keeps a firm grip while his grandfather struggles to right himself.

Everything is all right. Granddad has nothing to worry about. Nothing at all. After all, Tim is here.

SEVEN

Absolutely Useless

Granddad settles into the opposite end of the raft, still giggling in ragged bursts, and takes charge of the oars.

"We're off," Tim says.

Granddad says it, too. "We're off." Then he adds, "Like a turd of hurtles."

"Like a herd of turtles," Tim repeats. It's another of their jokes.

Tense, Tim watches as Granddad jerks the oars, but after a few stuttering tries, he gets a rhythm going and Tim begins to relax. The raft glides along the surface of the water, moving away from the shore, heading unerringly for their favorite spot for walleye fishing on the other side of the lake. It's a spit of land that extends out into the water. Fish tend to congregate on the windward side of the spit. They've always had especially good luck getting walleye there.

Tim settles against the air-cushioned side of the raft and sighs. Everything is going to be all right. Everything *is* all right. He knows the lake. Granddad knows the lake, too. And the plan is going to work. Grandma, Mom, Paul, all of them will have to admit that a man who can still drive to Silver Lake, row a boat, and go fishing doesn't belong in a nursing home.

Maybe he and his grandfather don't even need to stay on to camp and live off the land the way they've been talking about. Once they have caught a few fish, their point will be made, and then they can head back home. Mom and Grandma are probably worried enough by now. When he and Granddad walk in, they'll be ready to do some serious listening.

For now, though, there is nothing to do but to enjoy being here with Granddad. Enjoy being here and catch some fish.

Tim gazes at the trees probing the sky, at their dark reflections stretching into that other sky floating on the surface of the lake. A *V* of Canada geese fly over, calling and calling. "Are you there?" the call asks. "I'm here. I'm here," comes the answer.

"They always put me in mind of donkeys braying," Granddad says.

"I think they sound more like squeaky doors," Tim replies.

Granddad pulls the oars and lifts them, pulls and lifts. And Tim is content. How can he be anything else? He is home. No one will ever take him away from his grandfather again.

If Mom and Paul won't move back to Sheldon, then they'll have to understand that he must stay. He'll miss them both, especially his mother, and he knows they will miss him, but they can come back to visit often.

When the raft approaches the windward side of the spit, at a nod from his grandfather, Tim drops the anchor. When he hands over the pole, Granddad examines the way it is rigged, then gives another nod, clearly satisfied. Tim's chest swells with pride.

Granddad selects a particularly active minnow, slips his hook through behind the spine and drops his line in. Tim does the same. They each let the weight settle to the bottom, then reel about a foot of line back in. That way the minnow can swim freely.

All this has been done in silence, but they never fish in complete silence. Some fishermen say that any conversation at all will scare the fish away, but Tim and his grandfather have always talked when they are sitting with poles in their hands, and it's rare that they don't get fish. It's the talk Tim loves, perhaps even more than the fishing. He waits to see what the topic will be.

"Did you know," Granddad says finally, his voice a familiar low melody, "that fish have a sense we don't?"

Tim smiles, shakes his head. No, he didn't know. That's one his grandfather hasn't told him. But even if he had heard it before, he would be glad to hear it again.

"They have dots running down the sides of their bodies—it's called a lateral line system— and those dots help them sense what's around them in the water." Granddad settles back against the side of the raft. He looks relaxed, happy. "Sometimes two male fish will swim side by side, flapping their tails. They're trying to control their territory, shouting at each other's lateral line systems."

All Tim's life his grandfather has dropped bits of information like this on him, mostly about the natural world. That bats hunt with high cries we cannot hear. That bees see ultraviolet, invisible to us. That we humans have nine muscles to move our ears, and that those muscles usually don't work. That dogs have seventeen that work just fine.

"Did you know," Tim replies, because he's been gathering facts of his own to carry back to his grandfather, "that one of an owl's ear holes is higher than the other? That makes it so an owl can tell the height of a mouse by the sound it makes."

Granddad holds up a thumb to make an "all right" sign. They grin at each other.

A great blue heron standing near the shore thrusts its elegantly long beak into the water and comes up with a flapping fish. "Good work there, Blue," Granddad calls softly. Then they both turn back to study their lines as though concentration can help the minnows in their work below.

Tim reels in his line, checks his minnow—still active, still good—and drops it in again. A couple of minutes later, Granddad does the same.

There are other topics Tim wants to talk about, though, topics that have nothing to do with animals. For instance, why did Granddad quit his practice? He had been the best veterinarian in three counties. Everybody said that. The farmers used to call him from miles around to come care for their animals. People drove long distances to bring their pets to the clinic, too.

No one knew why, in the midst of prepping for surgery one day, Granddad had walked out of the clinic, gone home, marched in the front door and, without saying a word to anyone, sat down and started to read the newspaper. When Grandma asked him what he was doing home at that time of day, he'd said, "I'm reading the newspaper. Can't you see?" And he's never given any more of an explanation than that. As far as Tim knows, no one has ever dared to ask again. Not even his grandmother.

Tim studies the point where his line disappears into the water, gazes so intently that the shimmer of light on the surface begins to dazzle his eyes. He speaks without looking away or even blinking. "Why did you quit?" he asks. "Being a veterinarian, I mean."

The silence in the raft stretches like a taut rubber band. And stretches and stretches. Just when Tim is sure something must snap, Granddad says, "Do you know how you can tell the age of a bear at a glance?"

Tim sighs. He knows. He doesn't mind being told something that he's heard before, but for a moment there, he had actually thought he was going to get an answer to his question. He puts a finger beneath his line and gives it a tug, though they aren't really set up for jigging. "No," he says. "How can you tell?"

"By the size of the ears." Granddad is triumphant the way he always is when he thinks he's come up with a fact Tim doesn't know. "Even after a bear is grown, its skull keeps growing. But the ears stay the same. So when you look at an old bear, the ears seem smaller than they are on a young one. They aren't really, of course. They're just small in comparison to the head."

Tim nods. He wishes he had another piece of information to offer in exchange, but he doesn't. He's going to have to go to the library when he gets back to Minneapolis. They've got dozens of books about animals there. But then he remembers—he's not going back to Minneapolis. Well, he'll see if the Sheldon library has anything new.

"A bear's penis keeps growing, too," Granddad says. "It's made of bone, and the older he gets, the bigger it is."

Tim can feel the blood rush to his face. He's never heard his grandfather talk dirty. But then maybe to a veterinarian talk about an animal's penis isn't dirty. Granddad has never said such a thing to him before, though.

Having nothing to contribute to the conversation about bears' penises, Tim searches for another topic. He is almost surprised at what comes tumbling out. "Tell me about my father."

"Your father?" Granddad repeats, almost as though he doesn't know who Tim is talking about. His gaze is steady on his line.

Tim can't help but feel impatient. "You know. Your son, Franklin. Tell me about him."

"Ah . . . Franklin." Granddad's voice is so filled with love that Tim could almost warm his hands at it. "What do you want to know?"

Why did he go away? Tim thinks, but remembering his grandfather's studied lack of response to his other "why" question, he chooses safer ground instead, "Did he like to fish? You said you used to bring him out here to Silver Lake."

Granddad reels his lure in, picks a tangle of lake weed off the minnow, and casts again to a slightly different spot. Just when Tim is certain he isn't going to answer this question either, he says, "I used to bring Franklin here sometimes. I don't know that he ever liked fishing all that much, though."

"He didn't like it?" How could anyone not like going fishing? Especially with Granddad!

"It required too much sitting for his taste. Now, if I could have given him a spear, sent him into the lake after the fish, I think he would have liked that just fine." Granddad smiles, but the smile seems sad.

Fishing with his grandfather has always been Tim's favorite thing in all the world to do. The thought that his father didn't like it seems to put a thousand miles of distance between them. How could he not have liked just being out here on the silken water with Leo Palmer, whether he cared about fishing or not?

For several moments Granddad says nothing more. Then, as though Tim has asked another question, he adds, "Franklin always wanted me to take him hunting instead. I should have done it, I suppose."

Hunting. Another thousand-mile distance. Many of Tim's friends in Sheldon hunt with their fathers. They come back boasting of their kills, of the blood and guts they saw. Jeff Kowalski even invited Tim to come along once, but Tim made up an excuse. The truth is he didn't want to go. He wouldn't mind getting a chance to shoot a gun. That would be fun. But he could never shoot at anything alive.

It took a long time before he'd been able to take a fish off a hook, cut off the head and scrape the silvery scales and gut it without almost turning inside out himself. Granddad says he's got a tender stomach. Mom says he's got a tender heart. Whichever part of him is tender, the idea of looking into a deer's liquid eyes and pulling a trigger, of killing frightened little rabbits or the geese that fly overhead, calling in those lonely voices, has never appealed to him one little bit.

But his father liked hunting, actually wanted to go. Would a man who liked hunting, who didn't want to sit still to fish, have liked him?

The tip of Granddad's pole trembles, then tugs toward the water. Once. Twice. They both go still, watching the pole intently. And then the tip draws down again and stays arched toward the water. Granddad flashes a triumphant look in Tim's direction and begins reeling in.

"You've got a good one!" Tim whispers the exclamation, though noise probably couldn't disrupt anything now, and begins immediately to reel his own line in to get it out of the way. He discards his minnow, which is beginning to look the worse for wear, secures the hook in one of the eyes of the pole, and locks the reel.

"The net," Granddad says.

Tim lays his pole down and looks around.

No net. Granddad forgot to put the net into the raft. *He* forgot as much as Granddad did, though Granddad has always taken care of such details before. What a stupid thing to do, to go out fishing without a net!

Granddad is reeling in steadily, and Tim looks around, trying to see something else that can help land the fish. There is nothing.

His grandfather has his catch close to the raft now, and his pole is bent almost double. The fish is swimming hard, this way and that. Swimming for its life. Tim can see the dark back, the spiny dorsal fin. It's a walleye, all right. A big one. Ten pounds. Maybe more. It's been a long time since they've seen a walleye this big.

"Old Marble Eyes," Granddad cries. "It's Old Marbles Eyes. Bring me that net!"

"Sorry," Tim says, moving toward his grandfather, his hands empty. "We forgot." He leans over the side for a better look. He can see the long greenish back. A prize fish for sure. The kind to stuff and mount and hang on the wall. If Grandma were the kind to allow stuffed fish to be hung on her walls. "We didn't bring the net."

"What?" Granddad's voice is sharp.

"I'm sorry," Tim repeats. He doesn't add, as he might, *I'm sorry you forgot to put it in the raft*.

"Dammit, boy. Can't you do anything right?"

The words explode from Granddad's mouth, and Tim's head jerks up. His grandfather has never spoken to him this way before. Rarely even been angry with him. Certainly never sworn at him. Not in all his life.

"Everything," his grandfather is saying. "I have to do everything myself." His eyes are icy blue, fierce.

"It's not . . ." Tim starts, but he can't finish. *It's not my fault* is what he means to say. *You're the one who's supposed to be in charge.* But he looks at the dark color staining his grandfather's face, at the anger setting his mouth in deep parentheses, and he doesn't dare say it.

Granddad drops his pole and takes the line in his hand instead, moving in closer to the big walleye. "Not only can you not sit still long enough to catch a fish, but you can't manage to take any responsibility, either. Never known how. Never will." He spits the words as, with a single, strong pull, he lifts the walleye out of the water. The magnificent specimen rises straight up along the side of the raft. Tim sees what is going to happen. He sees and might have cried out a warning, but he does not.

The walleye hasn't swallowed the hook. The minnow is still there, a flash of silver in the big fish's mouth. And once Old Marble Eyes is half out of the water, he spits it. Just lets the minnow go and drops back into the lake. Slips into the water like someone sliding into bed. Without a farewell glance. Without even a splash.

For several long seconds, Tim's grandfather stares at the surface of the water. Stares at the ripple widening and widening. And then slowly he turns to face Tim again. Tim sees, as though from a great distance, that his grandfather's face is twisted with rage. "You're useless," he cries. "I don't know why I bother to bring you here. You're absolutely useless!" And he jerks the empty line out of the water.

Before Tim can gather any kind of response, he hears a new sound. One he has never heard before. Not out here in the raft, anyway. Nonetheless, he knows instantly what it is. He would have recognized that sound in his dreams.

A hissing. A fizzing. A sharp release of air. And he looks to see what has happened. When Old Marble Eyes spit the minnow, the minnow must have come free of the hook, too. Now the bare hook is caught in the side of the raft, puncturing the top chamber. The largest tube. The one that gives the raft its shape, its lift above the water. And around the penetrating hook, the air rushes out in a savage whisper.

See? the hissing air says. *See? You're absolutely useless, Timothy Palmer!*

EIGHT

Disaster!

Tim's grandfather kneels, studying the slowly collapsing side of the raft. He seems calm, almost mesmerized by the disaster overtaking them.

"Granddad!" Tim cries, lifting the dripping anchor out of the water and dropping it to the floor of the raft. "You've got to do something."

His grandfather reaches out to touch the deflating chamber, but he says nothing, does nothing.

"Row!" Tim shouts, rising to his knees.

For a moment, Granddad's attention shifts to the oars, and Tim thinks he is going to pick them up and begin to use them, but he doesn't. He only stares at them, then at Tim, his mouth half open.

"Please," Tim pleads.

But Granddad buries his face in his hands.

Tim looks down at the dark water lapping hungrily at the side of the raft. His eyes measure the distance to shore. Then he takes in the curled lump that is his grandfather. Exasperated—disgusted, really—he crawls past him until he is in a position to reach the oars himself. He gives his grandfather a light push. "Change places with me," he commands.

His grandfather doesn't budge.

Tim reaches past him for one of the oars, then the other. As he works, he can feel the heat climbing his neck, tingling his scalp. *Useless*, is he? He'll just see who's useless! If anyone around here is useless, it's his grandfather. Tim can't even row properly with him in the way.

He lifts a foot and gives his grandfather another push, a real shove this time, and Granddad topples onto his side, his knees still drawn up, his face still buried. Lying there, he reminds Tim of the pictures he's seen of a fetus, as if he's pretending to be a baby that's not even born. At least he isn't obstructing the oars so much now, and Tim can begin to row. They have another problem, though. Granddad's head now rests on the deflating top chamber, pushing it down so lake water runs into the raft in a steady stream.

Is he ever this bad around Grandma? If he is, no wonder she sounds so cross all the time.

"Granddad, you've got to move!" Tim shouts.

"You're letting water into the raft. You've got to get up and go sit in the back."

To his surprise and relief, his grandfather gathers himself enough to do as he is told. He crawls to the back of the raft and sits there, hugging his knees to his chest. With his head no longer pressing down the collapsing side, the water stops pouring in, but there is nothing to do about what has already collected in the bottom of the raft. It sloshes back and forth, wetting Tim's sneakers, the seat of his jeans. Granddad is getting soaked, too. In fact, he is wetter than Tim, because until he moved he'd been lying in the water that was pouring in. For so early in the fall, the lake is surprisingly cold.

Tim pulls as hard as he can on the oars. One dips deeper than the other, turning the raft in the water without moving them toward the shore. Tim positions himself more carefully and pulls on the oars again. This time the raft moves, just barely. He can't remember ever being so angry, especially with his grandfather. He can hardly remember a time when he has been angry with his grandfather at all.

Useless. Of all the unfair accusations! Hasn't he always been Granddad's best helper? Hasn't Granddad told him he is?

Tim digs at the water again. The deflated fabric of the top chamber has flattened to the point that it is hanging into the water. The air, instead of escaping with a hiss, sends up a silent stream of bubbles. As the top chamber sinks farther, water trickles over the collapsing side into the bottom of the boat with each pull of the oars.

"I'm sorry," Granddad moans. His face is buried against his knees, and his words comes out muffled.

"What?" Tim barks. He heard, but he wants to hear it again. The man *ought* to be sorry, that's for sure.

Granddad lifts his head and looks directly at Tim. "I'm sorry, Franklin," he says.

The hairs along Tim's arms rise. *Franklin!* As though Tim's father has suddenly appeared, as though he is sitting right there in the middle of the raft, in the deepening puddle which occupies the space between Tim and his grandfather.

Why does Granddad think he needs to apologize to Franklin, anyway? Doesn't he remember that Franklin is the one who went away? Years and years ago he walked out. By his own choice. Even though Tim left, too, that was different. He hadn't wanted to go. His mother and Paul had made him.

Besides, he's here now, isn't he? Listening to those old, old stories, sitting perfectly still to fish—getting yelled at. Taking over in a disaster.

Tim pulls hard on the oars, but this time the raft bumps against something and wallows there, water sloshing back and forth in the channels of the raft's floor. Have they reached the shore already? He looks over his shoulder.

No shore. That is still a good hundred feet away. What they have come up against is a stand of wild rice. The water between them and the shore is clogged with the long grass, the stems too thick to row through. If they were in a canoe, they could slip between the tall plants, but the raft is too wide to fit.

He looks both directions along the stand of rice. It seems to go on forever without a break. He can't tell how far. They've never come to shore here before, because if they did, they'd be on the opposite side of the lake from where they always camp. He'd like to try rowing back across the way they came, but he doesn't dare. What is left of the raft won't sink, but it's certainly not going to keep them dry. By the time the air is completely out of the top chamber, it's going to be pretty hard to maneuver, too.

He turns the raft and begins moving along the

edge of the wild rice bed. Already the rowing is getting hard. The water they are taking on increases the weight of the boat, and his shoulders and arms ache. There is no point in expecting any kind of help, though. His grandfather is sitting there, staring at him as if he doesn't know who he is. Which is, undoubtedly, the truth.

"I'm sorry," Granddad says again. "I didn't mean . . ." His voice trails off, leaving whatever he didn't mean dangling in the air.

He's talking to Franklin still. Tim knows that now. He must have thought Tim was Franklin when he yelled at him earlier, too. Well, who cares if he wants to sit in a puddle of cold water, talking to someone who isn't even there? Who hasn't been there for years.

Who cares about anything at all?

His grandfather shivers, a shudder so violent Tim almost expects to hear his bones rattle.

Tim keeps rowing. He can see what looks like an opening in the tall grass just a little farther down the shore. Wide enough, it seems, to bring the crippled raft to shore. The air in the boat is so diminished now that it buckles with each stroke, and with each stroke more cold water gushes in.

Granddad's teeth are clattering like castanets. "Sophie," he moans. "I want Sophie."

"You'd better not wish for Grandma," Tim warns through clenched teeth. "She's going to be mad at you. Plenty mad at you by now. Just like me."

But his grandfather doesn't seem to hear. He just whimpers again, "Sophie!"

NINE

No Choice

By the time Tim noses the collapsing raft up to the shore, he is shivering, too, though the spasms that set his teeth chattering seem to come from a deeper cold than the one in the air. How dare his grandfather say such things to him . . . and then turn around and pretend he's here with Franklin? How dare he sit there doing nothing and leave Tim to save the situation?

And what are they going to do now? They are on wrong side of the lake.

Tim looks longingly across the lake. If only he'd been able to row back to their campsite. Then they could climb right into the camper and drive home.

The bank here is steep, too steep to bump the raft onto the shore, so Tim steps out into the water, still in his shoes. At least he's wearing canvas sneakers that won't be ruined.

"Come on." He says it roughly and reaches a hand out to help his grandfather.

Ignoring the offered hand, Granddad throws his legs over the side of the raft and steps into the water. Tim notices, grimly, that his grandfather's lips are blue.

Serves him right if he's cold, he thinks. *Serves him right!*

When they step up onto the land, Granddad makes no attempt to assist Tim with the boat. He just clambers up the bank and stands at the top, gazing off into the forest. After several attempts to get the raft up the steep bank by himself, Tim gives up and ties it to a sapling. He leaves the tackle box in the bottom of the boat. They have a long walk ahead of them, and the tackle box is heavy. Besides, Granddad probably wouldn't help with that, either.

His grandfather doesn't seem to notice that Tim is leaving anything important behind. He just starts out walking, taking the lead and moving around the end of the lake toward their campsite on the other side. At least he knows the route. Though any baby could make it to their campsite with the shore of the lake to follow. The sun is sliding down the sky, approaching the tops of the trees, but they should have plenty of light to find their way back.

Off in the woods, something *rat-a-tat-tats*

against the trunk of a tree. Loud enough to be a jackhammer. Must be a pileated woodpecker. They are the only ones big enough to make that much noise.

Tim isn't sure why he's so furious, even now that he realizes Granddad was yelling at Franklin before, not at him. Maybe he's angry because it is so apparent that his grandfather is leaving. As surely as if he walked out the door, he is going away.

Maybe he's angry because . . . But he doesn't know. He doesn't care. The anger just sweeps through him, and he opens himself to it as to a cleansing wind.

The trek through the forest is rough. An occasional path created by deer or by anglers goes directly to the lake, not around it. At least the woods they are moving through are dense enough that there is not much undergrowth, but the trees themselves crisscross the ground with knobby roots. Occasionally they come to a windfall, too, and have to crawl over or make their way around the rotting trunk.

Granddad keeps moving. He doesn't even glance back to see whether Tim is following.

When they get back to the camper, they can get warm. They can have a sandwich, too, and some hot chocolate. No. No hot chocolate. Granddad forgot to take on water. Though perhaps they could boil some water from the lake. Is there anything dangerous in the water that wouldn't be killed by boiling? Tim doesn't think so, but he's not sure. Can he trust his grandfather to answer a question like that?

As soon as they are warm and fed and rested, they will drive back home.

Tim studies his grandfather's back. His gait is unsteady. He stumbles often. He will be able to drive when they get back to the camper, won't he?

Bullfrogs croak from the edge of the lake. They sound like string instruments in a school orchestra, clumsily tuning up. As Tim and his grandfather approach, the frogs go silent. Tim wants to stop, to wait for them to start up again, but the sun is below the tops of the trees now. Granddad doesn't slow his stumbling progress, anyway.

A noisy red squirrel on a branch above their heads tosses down an acorn, then another. Tim wonders whether the little creature is harvesting for winter or warning the human intruders away. Tim wouldn't mind being a small squirrel himself, with acorns to throw.

A bird Tim can't see whistles a descending tune, like a boatswain's whistle. A white-throated sparrow? He would ask his grandfather, but what does Granddad know? Birds are Grandma's territory.

And then he understands. In an instant, he realizes what has made him so angry. It is the way his grandfather talked . . . thinking he was talking to Franklin. The things he said. The manner in which he said them.

Useless! He must have talked to his own son that way. No wonder Franklin went away and refused to come back. No wonder he'd had "problems"!

"You were mean to my father." Tim aims the accusation at his grandfather's back.

It's just a guess. No one has ever suggested anything of the kind. Except maybe for the few times when Granddad had gotten really angry with Tim. The minute his voice went up in volume, Grandma would cut him off. "Are you going to start that again?" she'd say, her own voice heavy with meaning. Until now, Tim had never understood what she meant.

But now he is absolutely certain that his guess is right. Granddad didn't get along with his son. Didn't even like him, from the way he'd sounded.

He calls again to his grandfather's back. "You used to yell at Franklin, didn't you? You used to call him names."

This last stops Granddad abruptly. He turns to face Tim, but he doesn't look at him. He doesn't respond to his accusations, either.

Tim has lived too long in the silence about his father. Too long with the adult lies. *Nobody knows why he left, Tim. We don't have any idea why he would do such a thing.*

"No wonder my father didn't want to stay," he says "if that's the way you used to talk to him!"

Granddad doesn't defend himself, doesn't move. He just stands there with his head bowed, his arms hanging loosely at his sides.

"It's your fault."

"It's my fault," his grandfather agrees, though his voice is so flat, so without feeling the words seem almost to have lost their meaning.

Even though Tim said it first, even though he'd known it before he said it, he is stunned. "What did you do to him?" he asks when he can speak again. "Did you tell him he was useless?" The question is almost a whisper.

Granddad sighs deeply, as though he finds the entire discussion intensely wearying. He replies, still without any feeling that Tim can detect, "Yes. I told Franklin he was useless."

"No wonder he left." Tim can barely say the words.

Granddad fixes Tim with those mild blue eyes and replies simply, "He had no choice. I told him he had to go."

Tim stands still as a deer caught in the glare of approaching headlights, though his head is reeling. *Had to go? He told my father he* had *to go!* He reaches out to support himself on the trunk of a nearby sapling.

"But why? Tell me why."

He waits, as though by merely standing there he can force his grandfather to answer. He knew, though, even as he asked the question, that no answer would come. And he was right.

His grandfather has already turned and, weaving a bit, is walking again.

"He must have hated you!" Tim shouts after the retreating back. "My father must have hated you. Do you know that?"

His grandfather doesn't answer that question, either. He just keeps walking, keeps moving ahead around the rim of the lake until the trees and the occasional low bushes close in behind him, obscuring him from view.

Tim waits until even the crackle of twigs, of dry leaves beneath his grandfather's feet is silenced. Then he begins walking, too.

He was right. He supposes he should feel good about that. He was right.

But he has never felt worse in his life.

TEN

Where Are You?

Home! Tim touches the side of the camper almost reverently. The walk was so long—the hike around the end of the lake must have taken at least an hour—that he'd begun to wonder if he was ever going to see their campsite and the old pickup camper again.

The last of the sunset has drained from the sky over the lake. Silver, then pewter, now charcoal gray. Soon the sky will be a dark navy blue . . . on its way to black. There is no sign of a moon yet.

Tim scans the campsite. No sign of his grandfather, either. He walked on ahead at a steady enough pace that Tim never caught up with him. Not that he tried.

The old man is probably inside the camper already, eating his stinky salami.

Tim wraps his arms around himself and shivers. The wind has grown stronger, more insistent, instead of dropping as it so often does around sunset. The lake is dotted with whitecaps. The air is definitely cooler. Tim's jeans are wet, his feet, too, and even parts of his sweatshirt. On a night like this, his clothes would barely be enough to warm if they were dry.

He steps away from the camper. What will he say to his grandfather? What is there left to say except to repeat the question. *Why? Why did you send my father away?*

Would it make any difference, even if he answered? Leo Palmer abused his son, yelled at him, called him names. He admitted that he did. And then, just when someone was on his way into the world who was really going to need Franklin, he told him to leave. What was wrong with the man?

He would never forget that his grandfather did that. Never forget and never forgive.

A gust sets the trees creaking and moaning overhead, brings waves to slap at the shore.

Tim shivers again. He has to go in there and face his grandfather. What will he say to him? What is there left to say to him? No wonder everyone has been so reluctant all these years to talk about Franklin, to say anything about him at all. Talking about him might have forced them to admit the truth, that Granddad was to blame for Tim's never having seen his father . . . even once. For his father's never having seen him.

Tim moves around to the camper door. Funny that Granddad is in there without a light. There is no electric hookup at this campground, but they always used to keep a gas lantern tucked away in the cupboard, and it must be dark enough inside to need it now.

As soon as they both have something to eat, Granddad can drive back to Sheldon, back to the house. Once the grownups are through with the fit they're sure to throw—funny how quickly people can go from scared to angry—Tim will tell them the truth. And the truth is that he's ready to go home. Back to Minneapolis. Back with his mother and with Paul.

Granddad doesn't need him here anymore. If anything is clear, that is.

Besides, Granddad has no one to blame but himself. Even if he does have Alzheimer's, he can't use that as an excuse for the way he treated his son. Franklin has been gone for years!

Tim shakes himself. Why is he standing out here, getting colder and colder? And what is he afraid of, anyway? Certainly not a forgetful old man.

94

But when he steps onto the bottom step and puts his hand on the doorknob, just lays his palm on the cold metal, he doesn't even try to turn it. Because he knows.

His grandfather isn't in there. The camper is too quiet. The windows are too dark. Even the wind that had been rushing about a moment before is suddenly too still. But since there is nothing else to do, he turns the handle anyway. Or tries to turn it.

The door is locked.

Tim steps back down to the uneven ground and scans the darkening campground. Empty. He and his grandfather are the only campers here. They haven't seen another soul since they left Melvin's.

Where else could Granddad have gone? He was walking ahead, following the lake. Even he couldn't get lost in the woods following the perimeter of the lake.

Tim executes a slow circle, searching the campground again. His gaze falls on the out-house in the center of the loop of campsites, a rustic building designed to blend in with the landscape. Except for the smell. That never quite "blends."

Tim smiles at the thought, and the cold certainty of disaster that has been clutching at his throat loosens its hold. The outhouse. That's where Granddad is, of course. He'll be back any moment now. All Tim has to do is wait. He sinks slowly to the camper steps, uncertain whether he has chosen to sit or if his knees have simply given way.

What would he have done if Granddad had truly been gone? If he'd found himself alone in this forest? He won't even think about that. He can't.

A pale egg-shaped moon rises from behind the trees on the other side of the lake. It lightens the surrounding sky, glimmers on the surface of the water. But beneath the trees surrounding the camper, the shadows only grow more dark.

Tim scuffs at the ground with the heel of his wet sneaker. His shoes aren't sodden any longer, but they are certainly far from dry. His clothes adhere to his skin with a clammy grip. The night air is damp, too, so that the persistent wind is little use in drying them.

Why is the old man taking so long?

Old man. He's never used such language about his grandfather before. Not even in his mind. But then he has never felt about him the way he feels today.

How could Granddad have treated his own son that way?

And why is he taking so long in the outhouse?

After another long minute, Tim gets up and heads for the privy. He'll knock on the door, tell him to hurry. If he, Tim, could only drive—if he even had a clue about driving, especially a truck with a stick shift—he would take himself home and leave Granddad dreaming in the stink house. That's what the two of them have always called it, the stink house.

But as he approaches the privy, his steps grow increasingly leaden. Is it possible that he is wrong about his grandfather being there, too?

He stops in front of the outhouse door, closes his eyes, pleads under his breath. "Please. Let him be here." He doesn't know who he is talking to, really. Whoever it is out there who invented Alzheimer's disease?

Tim knows, even before the door rasps open, releasing the dark smell hiding behind it, that his plea won't be answered, and he is right.

The privy is empty.

He slams the door and turns back, his gaze skimming the shadowy campground. Where is Granddad? Where could he be? He couldn't have gotten lost on the way back to their campsite. That isn't possible.

Unless he didn't want to get back to the campsite.

Unless hearing those words—"He must have hated you. Do you know that?"—made him want to be lost.

Tim's heart pounds. His breath comes in short gasps.

Half running, half stumbling, he heads back to the camper. Maybe the door isn't really locked! Maybe his grandfather is there by now.

But, of course, he is wrong yet again. The handle won't turn. And when he pounds on the door, there is no response. Tim leans his forehead against the cold metal, trying to breathe, trying to think. A mournful hoot sounds from the branch just over his head, and he jumps away from the camper, letting out a small, strangled scream.

Can the owl tell from hearing him that he's too tall to be a mouse?

He wants to run. Anywhere. Everywhere. But he forces himself to stand instead, forces his breathing to slow. "It's all right," he says, speaking out loud. "Just be still. Everything is all right." It's what his grandfather used to say to his animal patients when they were frightened. "Be still now. Everything is all right."

Tim's hammering heart is the last to obey the order.

What should he do? He can't search the forest. Can't even begin. It stretches for miles and miles all around. He doesn't even have any idea how many miles. Grown men have gotten lost in there, hunters who go into the forest in full daylight with compasses and topographical maps and guns, with all kinds of aids for surviving, for finding their way out again. There is only one direction he knows for certain, the gravel road that leads out, that leads back to Melvin's.

It is several miles back to Melvin's store. Five or six, at least. Two or three miles to reach the edge of the forest. Another two or three to the corner and Melvin's store. And Tim is already cold and hungry and tired.

His grandfather must be cold and hungry and tired, too. Probably even more than he is.

Will Granddad die in the forest? Is that what he wants, to die?

A whimper escapes, forces its way out between Tim's lips. *I didn't mean. I didn't . . .*

The silent shadow passing over him sends him into a crouch, his arms over his head for protection.

He rises slowly. Granddad would laugh, seeing him this way. Afraid of an owl. Afraid not even of the owl but of the owl's shadow.

"Granddad." The cry is thin, useless, only another tremor in the rising wind. "GRAND-DAD! WHERE ARE YOU?"

ELEVEN

Found

He might have been walking for hours. It probably hasn't been that long, but Tim's feet and legs ache, and the night has grown so black that the stars are bright pinholes in the shroud of the sky. If it weren't for the moon, he would have trouble even making out the boundaries of the narrow gravel road he has been following. As it is, the faint light is insufficient to keep him from stepping into a rut now and then. He has turned his left ankle twice, and now it throbs.

He walks on, almost relishing the pain. It takes his mind off the thunder rumbling in the distance. Off the way his sodden jeans chafe his skin. Off the rawness of his throat when he calls, again and again, "Granddad!" It almost takes his mind off the silence that comes back to him after each call . . . like an accusation.

How could he have spoken to his grandfather

that way? How could he have let him go on ahead? How could he even have encouraged him to go camping? He came here to help, but he has made everything worse.

Whatever happened between his grandfather and Franklin, Granddad has always been good to him.

He attended every father-son scout banquet Tim ever was involved in, even when he had to close the clinic early to do it. He was always at his Little League games, too. He taught Tim to fish, to build a campfire, to roll a sleeping bag so small it could actually be stuffed back into its original bag.

When Grandma wasn't looking, he even used to sneak Tim ripe olives from the table while they were enduring the endless wait for holiday dinners.

"Granddad!" he calls again.

A dark shape lumbers across in front of him, several yards down the road. Tim stops abruptly, peering after it. A bear? No, too small for a bear. Too big to be anything he wants to meet, though. Probably a raccoon. He shivers. Raccoons' masked faces are comical, appealing, but something about their profile, the rounded back, the lowered head, makes them sinister. He would almost rather encounter a bear. The black bears they have here in Wisconsin rarely bother people.

He wonders if a bear's penis really is bone. But Granddad said it is, so it must be.

For the first time, it occurs to him to wonder, too, what Franklin did to deserve being called "useless"—to deserve being sent away.

He sighs and looks off into the dense trees on each side of the road. Maybe he should have retraced his steps around the end of the lake instead of starting out on the road toward Melvin's. Could he possibly have passed his grandfather on the way back to the campground without seeing him?

Tim shakes his head, moves on. If he had gone back instead of heading out for the store, it would have taken him more than an hour to return to the place where he had tied the raft to the sapling. And he was pretty sure he wouldn't have found Granddad along the way if he had. Then he would have been left to walk the entire distance back to the campground again, this time in full dark, before being able to start for help. That's the important thing—to find help. He may be a dumb little kid, but he's not so dumb as to think this is a situation he can manage by himself.

He keeps walking. His feet feel like clumps of concrete. Wet concrete. Wet and cold.

He shouldn't have blamed Granddad for being

mean to Franklin. He knows nothing of what happened between the two of them, but he knows his grandfather. He is kind, gentle, fair. More than one of Tim's friends has told him how lucky he is to have Dr. Leo as a grandfather, as a father, really. And he'd never needed to be told.

"Granddad!" he calls.

Silence.

He puts one heavy foot in front of the other. When he doesn't hold his jaw tight, his teeth chatter in machine-gun bursts. Maybe he's going to die. It's silly to think about that, though. No one dies from a little bit of cold, a little bit of hunger, a little bit of being lost.

Granddad won't die, either.

Will he?

Besides, even if Granddad is lost, Tim isn't. He knows where he is. He knows where he's going. To Melvin's to get help for his grandfather. Being lost and having a long way to go are two entirely different things.

The wind sets the trees to groaning, rattles their leaves. The leaves sound dry, dead, though most of them haven't even begun to color yet. The whole world is rushing toward winter.

Off in the distance beyond the lake, lightning flashes. A mutter of thunder follows. Tim counts.

A thousand and one. A thousand and two . . . A thousand and seven. Seven seconds between the lightning and the thunder. That means the storm is seven miles away. Maybe it will pass by instead of coming this way. Maybe he'll be lucky, and the rain will rain itself out on some farmer's crops. But this is harvest time. The farmers probably don't want rain, either.

The road bends to the left and, coming around the curve, Tim stops abruptly, straining to see. There is a dark lump by the side of the road just ahead. Big enough to be a bear this time.

But what is a bear doing sitting there so still? Is he watching? Waiting for his dinner to come tripping by?

Tim gives himself a shake. Now he's being silly. But still, he can't seem to find the strength to start forward again. Maybe he should—But no. He's not going to turn back to the campground and the pickup truck. He has come too far. Besides, a locked camper is no good. He's on his way to get help. His grandfather is out there somewhere . . . needing him, counting on him, and he has to get help.

He puts one foot down, then the other, moving forward by inches, closer to the black lump. It doesn't stir.

Then he remembers. Never take a bear by surprise. Make noise. Any kind of noise. If bears know you're in the area, they'll move out on their own. They don't want an encounter any more than you do.

The first time Tim opens his mouth, nothing happens. A gargle. A squeak. Something between a frog and a mouse. Hardly a sound to frighten a bear.

The second time he manages to form the word on his tongue, to get it past his lips in a whisper. "Granddad."

The third attempt comes out as a shout. "GRANDDDAD!"

Silence. The black lump doesn't budge. But then Tim hears the sound. Not a bear's low growl, which is what he expects. This sound is softer, sadder.

Someone is sobbing.

For an instant this clear sign of human misery is more terrifying than the snarl of any bear. Tim freezes, his feet rooted to the gravel road, though he wants more than anything else he can think of to run. But then the moon, which has been slipping in and out of the gathering clouds, shines through once more. A figure takes shape, sitting on a large boulder by the side of the road. Pale sheen of hair. Pale hands. Even the lighter squares of the plaid shirt reflect the thin moonlight.

"Granddad," he says again, quietly this time. "You're here. At last." Clearly Granddad had been heading for Melvin's, too.

The sobbing doesn't stop, doesn't even diminish, and Tim walks slowly, tentatively toward the figure, as though his grandfather were, indeed, some wild animal who might startle at his approach. He crouches by the boulder and reaches out gently to touch the woolen sleeve.

To his relief, the sobbing subsides. Granddad straightens his back and stares at Tim, his eyes almost glowing in the half light. "Franklin," he says at last. "Have you come to rescue me?"

"Yes," Tim says. "I've come to rescue you."

Granddad continues to stare so intently that, for a moment, Tim thinks he must be beginning to understand. *Oh, of course,* he will say. *You are not Franklin.* But the close perusal doesn't bring Tim back to his grandfather's mind, because he says, "I'm an old man, Franklin. Old before my time. I'm not even a vet any longer. Did you know?"

"You'll always be a vet," Tim says.

"No." Granddad shakes his head. "No. I gave it

up. Had to. Almost killed a kitten. Belonged to a little girl." A spasm of shivers passes through him, but whether he is reacting to the cold or to the memory, Tim can't tell. "Pretty little thing, that kitten. I meant to spay it. All I meant to do. Caught myself with the needle in my hand, ready to put the poor creature down. That's when I knew."

Tim doesn't have to ask what his grandfather knew. He lowers himself to the boulder, too, waits for whatever will come next. They sit side by side, each wrapped in his own night.

"I'm worried about you," Granddad says finally, and though he hasn't used the name this time, Tim knows he is talking to Franklin still. "You've got to kick the coke." He peers directly into Tim's face, unblinking. "I told you you couldn't come home again until you were clean."

Coke? Clean? Tim can't make it out. Is his grandfather talking about drugs? Was Franklin on cocaine? Is that the "problem" everyone has mentioned? Someone should have told him. He had a right to know such a thing about his own father.

"I won't let you stay." Granddad shakes his head violently. "I won't let you do damage to that girl . . . to that baby. I won't . . ." He half rises from the boulder, but he doesn't get very far before dropping back again. Then he is weeping once more, his stocky shoulders shuddering, his breath coming in rough gulps.

"It's all right, Granddad," Tim says. "It's all right." And it is.

He puts both arms around his grandfather's solid shoulders and rocks him, rocks him.

T W E L V E

Home

The sunlight shining through the flaming top of the maple awakens Tim. When he opens his eyes, the first thing he sees is his old Winnie-the-Pooh bedspread folded across the bottom of the bed. He is home. *Home!*

He sits up, stretches cautiously. His muscles are sore from the rowing. Probably sore from sitting so long in the cold and the wet, too.

He doesn't know how long he and his grandfather sat on the boulder, waiting to be rescued. He knows that the storm arrived, soaked them both thoroughly, and moved implacably on. He knows that his grandfather cried sometimes and that he, Tim, held him.

He held him till the lights of the car appeared. Then Tim ran out into the gravel road, waving his arms, and the car came to a skidding stop and Paul leapt out, shouting, "Tim! Tim!" Only then had he started bawling.

And there was Mom in the front seat, blubbering, too.

She'd known, she'd said, she'd been absolutely certain. She'd told Grandma a hundred times that Tim would be taking good care of his grandfather.

And that was when he realized what he had known all along, too. That his mother and Paul would find him. That they would search and search, asking everyone they knew—even Dr. Hutchins, even crabby Melvin—until they figured out where the two of them had gone.

Tim lies back again. His gaze rests on the flaming tree beyond the window. The morning is windy, and one branch taps insistently against the roof. Will he ever push open the window, grab that branch, and climb down the maple, surprising everyone by walking in the front door? Probably not, but then there are some paths his father took that he doesn't have to follow.

A knock on the door, softer than usual. His grandmother has always had an uncanny knack of knowing the minute he is awake. She can be at the other end of the house—in fact, she probably was—and she knows when he opens his eyes.

"Come in, Grandma," he calls.

She comes in. She is wearing a yellow sweat suit, yellow and bright as the morning sunlight.

She stands looking down at him, her fists cocked on her hips. "So," she says, half accusation, half greeting, "you're awake."

"Yes," he agrees. "I'm awake."

Is she going to scold him now? Is she going to blame him for putting his grandfather at such risk? She has the right.

By the time Paul and his mother arrived, Tim was struggling to remember everything Granddad had ever told him about hypothermia. He'd tried to get his grandfather to walk, just to keep him warm, if not to make it all the way either to Melvin's or back to the camper, but Granddad had no strength left for walking. Tim had been as frantic as the adults must have been back home. He knew that one sign of hypothermia was confusion, but he didn't know if the cold had anything to do with the way Granddad was talking.

After a time, he had no longer known where they were. He forgot even about Franklin. Once he'd reached into the pocket of his wool shirt and pulled his hand out again. "That's my daddy," he'd explained, and he'd held the "picture" up for Tim to see. But his hands had been cupped around nothing.

Grandma inclines her head toward the foot of

the bed, and Tim moves his feet to make room. She settles on the bottom corner.

"How is Granddad?" he asks.

She folds her hands in her lap, studies them as though they might hold the answer to his question. Grandma is short and pleasantly round—*chubby*, she calls herself—but her hands are slender, her fingers, long. *A piano-player's hands*, she's always said. *A piano-player's hands on a body without a scrap of musical talent. One of nature's jokes.* Is Alzheimer's disease another of nature's jokes?

"He's pretty confused still," she says finally, "but he'll be better when he's fully rested. Any kind of stress seems to put him over the edge for a time." She peers at Tim from beneath her finely arched dark eyebrows, but she doesn't smile. He notices particularly that she doesn't smile.

He nods, enormously relieved.

Silence fills the room. Not a bad silence, but Tim has no idea what might be coming next. He doesn't even know what he would like to come next.

"Timmy," Grandma says.

He winces.

"Tim," she corrects herself, clearing her throat. "I don't know when I've been so glad to see anybody as I was to see you and your grandfather last night. I'd about decided I'd lost you both."

"Were you really glad to see Granddad?" He shouldn't challenge her, he knows—not after what he put her through—but the question was lying there on the tip of his tongue, waiting to be asked.

Her chin comes up. A soft, round chin, but when she thrusts it forward like that, it's a chin to contend with. "What do you mean by that, young man?"

"Granddad says you're going to send him to a nursing home."

Grandma stares at Tim, her eyes round and astonished. She must be surprised that he knows. "No one is sending anybody to a nursing home." She speaks slowly and deliberately.

Would she dare lie to him? Tim pushes himself up on one elbow. "But he heard you talking to Mom . . . about selling the house, about a place that will be better for him. I know he's forgetting things, but that doesn't mean he can't understand what people say right in front of him!"

Grandma nods, once, twice. "Is that why you ran off with him? Because you thought I was going to put him in a nursing home?"

"Yes." Tim waits, watching his grandmother's face for any sign of deception.

She sighs. "I *am* going to sell the house."

Tim flops back down in the bed, crosses his arms over his chest.

She takes hold of one of his feet through the covers, gives it a small shake. "Listen," she commands. "I am going to sell the house, but I'm not putting Leo in a nursing home. As long as I can manage, he'll stay with me."

"Where are you going, then?"

"To Minneapolis."

Tim comes bolt upright in the bed. "What?"

"We're moving to Minneapolis, your grandfather and I. Your mother has found some senior apartments close by where you live. They have people there who can help me care for your grandfather."

Tim drops back again. He can think of nothing to say.

Grandma begins to massage his foot through the covers. "But Timmy . . ."

This time he lets her get by with the name. Doesn't even make a face.

"It's not the apartment we're moving for. It's you. It's your mother and Paul . . . and especially you. He needs you. We both do." She looks at him steadily, gravely.

"After yesterday . . . you still want to be close to me?"

"Why wouldn't I?"

"I caused you lots of grief. I meant to cause you grief."

Grandma gives his foot a squeeze. "Timothy Palmer, if there's one thing I've come to know, it's that everyone makes mistakes in this life. What counts is whether or not we learn by the mistakes we make."

"Like Granddad did . . . learned from his mistakes with Franklin?"

She gives him a studying look. The look is trying to ascertain what he knows, but she doesn't ask. "Franklin was a . . . a difficult boy," she says at last. "He was restless. Impatient. Quick to anger. So different from his father . . . and so much the same. Leo tried hard, but yes, he made mistakes. We both did."

She smoothes back her dark hair, then folds her hands again, those lovely, long-fingered hands. She looks up at Tim. "But when you came along . . . well, you were a different boy, and we . . . we could be different, too. Do you understand?"

Tim nods. He thinks he understands. But there is one more question still. A question he seems to have waited all his life to ask. He sucks in a huge breath, and when he lets it out, the words come tumbling out with it. "Do you ever hear from him? Do you know where my father is now?"

For an instant Grandma's lips tremble. Then she swipes a hand across her mouth, restoring it to firmness, and answers briskly. "No. We never hear from Franklin. I have no idea where he might be. I only hope that he is . . . well."

Tim sighs. What did he expect? That his father was going to hear of Granddad's illness and come running home to help?

Grandma leans forward, peers into Tim's face. She speaks softly. "There's not a day, though, I don't think about him. Not a day I'm not grateful to him."

"Grateful!" Tim is amazed. "Why would you be grateful?"

"For bringing you to us," she says. And at last she smiles.

Tim stands in the doorway to his grandparents' room, watching his grandfather in the bed. He is lying on his back, asleep, his chest rising and falling in a peaceful rhythm. Tim tiptoes closer.

Granddad's eyelids are thin, almost translucent. The skin is smooth over his strong cheekbones. His nose is as finely carved as any eagle's beak. He could be some magnificent animal lying there sleeping, a bear, perhaps, or a lion.

Tim touches his arm—not to wake him, just to

know he is there—and his eyelids flutter, come open. He studies Tim solemnly for a moment, then asks, "Is it winter yet?"

Tim glances out the window to the maple, dropping its leaves so heedlessly. "Not yet, Granddad," he says. *It's coming soon*, he adds, only to himself. *Too soon.*

Granddad's eyelids drift closed again, and Tim starts to turn away. But his grandfather reaches out and captures his hand, drawing him back to the side of the bed.

"Did I ever tell you," he asks, "about the way we used to catch mice in Alaska?"

"No," Tim says with the smallest trace of a sigh. "You never told me."

And he is off, telling the story again. At one point he rises on an elbow, animated, flushed. When he gets to the part about throwing out the bucket of dead mice, Tim draws his hand away. Considering all the animals his grandfather has saved over the years, why is he stuck on this story?

With the story done, Granddad lets his head sink back to the pillow and his eyes drift closed. Tim starts for the door once more. Maybe later, maybe after his grandfather has had more rest, he'll be able to talk about something besides winter and dead mice. The voice stops him in the doorway.

"That was until I worked out a better way."

Tim turns back.

Granddad is grinning. "When it was my turn to set the trap, I didn't use the bucket." He props himself up again. "I just spread the peanut butter on slices of bread and left them in the middle of the floor by the door."

"But what good was that?"

Granddad chuckles. "That's what the fellows said. 'What good is that, Leo?' And I said, 'You just wait and see.'"

Tim moves closer.

"We went to bed and went to sleep. Slept fine. Not a single mouse came into the bunk room all night long. You know why?"

Tim is beginning to get the picture, but he shakes his head, lays a hand on his grandfather's shoulder.

"The mice spent the whole night nibbling that peanut butter. They were so busy licking that bread clean they had no time to bother us, and every single mouse went back to its nest in the morning, happy." Granddad's delight in his story is huge.

Tim smiles. He should have known! But as quickly as the story and his grandfather's pleasure in it arose, they recede once more. Granddad's head drops back to the pillow again, and when Tim looks down at the familiar face, it has gone pale, the eyes dark.

"Can you forgive me?" Granddad asks.

Forgive you for what? Tim wonders. *For saving all those mice? For protecting me from my drug-addicted father? For being there my whole life?*

But then it occurs to him to ask, "Do you know who I am?"

For a long moment, his grandfather doesn't answer, doesn't give the smallest sign. Tim wonders if he even heard the question. Finally, though, he shakes his head, and Tim's throat goes raw.

"I'm afraid," Granddad says, "I'm afraid I've forgotten."

Tim's shoulders sag. He tries on a wavering smile. Should he try to tell him?

But a gentle hand reaches out to touch Tim's face. "I only know . . ." The hand traces a line along Tim's jaw to his chin. "I know you are someone I love."

Tim's shoulders lift. When his grandfather is rested, he will remember Tim's name once more. Tim is certain of that. But for now—and even for that other time when Granddad might forget again—the love will do.

"I love you, too," Tim says. "You know that I love you."

120